THE
END

THE
END

The End

by

Kayleigh Dobbs

BLACK SHUCK
SHADOWS

Black Shuck Books
www.BlackShuckBooks.co.uk

Cover design & internal layout © WHITEspace 2023
www.white-space.uk

First published in the UK by Black Shuck Books, 2023

978-1-913038-91-5

This collection is dedicated to Periphery, whose music takes me on epic imaginary journeys. The concept for this collection and every story in it is directly inspired by them, and wouldn't exist otherwise.

This book is also dedicated to Nick, my husband, who introduced me to Periphery and spent the last year giving me feedback on my ideas for these stories. I love you.

We come for war!

The Claim They Stake

Billy slipped halfway down the stairs. He tried to grip the banister to save himself but his hand slid right off it just as the heel of his foot shot off the next step, and he fell backwards, his shirt riding up as he bumped almost all the rest of the way down. He wouldn't feel the sting of the carpet graze on his back until later, when the adrenaline had worn off some. The bedroom door he had slammed shut behind him was flung open so hard it hit the wall. Billy screamed: it was the first genuine expression of terror he'd ever heard in his thirty-five years, and the fact that it came from him only exacerbated what was already an uncontrollable sense of panic.

Bare feet pounded across the floor above him as Billy landed at the bottom of the stairs. He windmilled his arms in a bid to propel himself upright, and then lunged across the small foyer towards the front door. His breath came out in ragged, uneven sobs as he reached for the door handle with one hand, and glanced at the other to make sure he hadn't dropped his phone. Ordinarily, his grip on the thing would have sufficed as proof that he was indeed still holding it, but it didn't strike him as stupid that he felt the need to check. It was a wonder the thing hadn't broken in his hand. Not that he would have turned back if he'd discovered that his hand was only grasping air. Old Mr. Tiley was right behind him.

Billy's hand slipped off the door handle once, twice, and a third time as he heard the same bare feet that had pursued him across the landing slap against the wall and continue sprinting down towards him. Billy screamed again, getting purchase on the handle but forgetting to push it down before trying to yank the door open. It rattled but held fast in its frame, mocking him.

Tiley's feet landed on the laminate flooring too close behind him, and just when Billy feared he would feel Tiley's breath on the back of his neck, the door swung open, and he was free. He expected to feel himself caught and yanked backwards to be swallowed first by the house and then by the thing residing within it, but he was across the road and in his own home less than twenty seconds later. He didn't look back once.

He turned so quickly to lock and chain the door that he pulled a muscle in his shoulder: a pain that would never have time to set in properly. His breath was escaping him in ragged puffs of air, his heart dancing in his ears and throat. Tears soaked his cheeks.

"Billy, what's wro... oh, careful!"

He half-turned at the sound of Maddie's voice and then he was falling over something. She lunged forward but didn't catch him in time, and had to settle for helping him up.

"Are you okay?" she asked, both her small hands gripping one of his as he clambered to his feet. Once he had finally righted himself, she offered him a tight-lipped smile and pulled her hands away, wiping his sweat off on the back of her jeans.

"They're here," he told her, moving past her into the living room. A live news reporter talked at him from the TV on the wall, something about a house in one of those posh areas inexplicably going up in a blazing ball of flames. Billy barely registered it. He was staring at the small screen in his own hand, frantically sending messages.

"Billy?" Maddie. Her voice was small, even for her. He barely heard her either. His fingers flew across the tiny touchscreen. He didn't notice that the love of his life was wiping away silent tears. That precarious final straw, which had been strained for some time, was about to snap.

He shoved his phone back into his pocket and paced in front of the sofa, undecided about whether or not to go through to the kitchen to grab the biggest knife he owned. He decided against it: his senses were returning to him now, and grabbing a carving knife would only freak Maddie out. Maybe the decorative sword hanging on the wall behind him, then? He often took it from its mantel and posed with it, usually to get a laugh out of her. She had no idea that he'd had it sharpened. Maybe the baseball bat he kept upstairs under their bed was the better option, the one he'd told Maddie was just there for safety in the event of a late-night break-in. He'd been careful in how he'd phrased that to ensure he wasn't lying as such, just omitting what exactly he was worried would break in.

"Who's here?" She'd followed him, but not all the way. She hovered in the living room doorway. "Billy!"

"Hmm?" He looked at her, wondering how she could still look so confused. It occurred to him that he hadn't yet voiced all of his erratic thoughts.

"Is he okay?" She blinked, utterly sweet and adorable in her ignorance and concern. He looked back at her blankly. She shook her head and sighed, moving into the room and towards the window. She looked out across the street. Then it dawned on him. She meant Mr. Tiley – that *thing* in the house he'd just fled from.

He lunged towards the window, knocking her aside as he yanked the curtains closed with almost enough force to pull the curtain pole down. His eyes started to sting and he swiped at them with his fingers, wiping away the sweat running down from his hairline. It struck him as funny, even in a moment like that, that he'd only just started sweating from anywhere but his palms now that he was calming down. It reminded him of when he used to go jogging – he'd sweat a little during the three miles or so but then would be drenched the moment he got home and sat down.

"Billy, you're freaking me out. Is he alright over there? Do we need to call someone?"

"He's one of them," he told her. "I was right about it all, and *he's* one of *them*."

He peered out of a gap in the curtains at Tiley's house to make sure he hadn't been followed. There was no one in the street. As he watched for signs of movement, he wondered how in the hell he was going to save them both from the onslaught that was inevitably coming their way.

He'd been looking for evidence of 'them' for years, but now that he had it, he wished he didn't. He wished he'd never gone to check on his old neighbour, and he wished he hadn't seen. Suspecting changed nothing, but *knowing* ruined everything.

They'd been accepting parcels for Mr. Tiley for a few days because the delivery people hadn't been getting an answer at his house. Billy had gone across the road and knocked a few times, but to no avail. Mr. Tiley was in his eighties and he never went anywhere for more than a day without asking Billy to water his plants. Finally, Bill became so worried that he considered calling the police. He'd decided to use the spare emergency key to check on the old man himself before alerting authorities, in case it turned out to be unnecessary. In any case, Tiley was a private guy and wouldn't appreciate his door being broken in by the police for all the neighbours to see, even if the worst had happened.

Billy had fetched the key that lived under Halpern, Tiley's favourite and largest garden gnome, and let himself in. It had been quiet apart from the hum of what Billy would discover were the several heat lamps in Tiley's bedroom. He went upstairs, calling for the old man but receiving no answer. It was hot and getting hotter as he reached the second floor and approached the only closed door. He knocked twice, called out, and upon hearing nothing back, he let himself in. And then he saw him in there.

Saw *it* in there.

"One of 'them'?" Maddie repeated. She opened her mouth to probe further and then cut herself off with a closed-eyed sigh. "Please, no. Not this again."

"Babe, we have to go somewhere, he knows I know."

"I knew you weren't done with this. I knew it."

"You didn't see it. He shed his..."

"You've been sneaking down here in the middle of the night and logging on to those forums again, haven't you?" She sounded hurt but unsurprised. "Billy, you promised me."

"We can just pack a case and go. Anywhere you want!" As the words left his mouth, something that had initially presented itself as a niggling question morphed into a prominent one. He moved past her and looked out to the front door of what he'd tripped over, the thing he'd been too distracted to pay attention to.

"Should have thrown that stupid laptop out of the window when you started getting obsessed with all this again." Maddie was slowly turning in his direction, her tiny frame ever smaller as she crossed her arms, hugging herself. "Are you even taking your medication anymore?"

"Why is there a suitcase by the door?" Logic told Billy that there was a much more pressing issue than Maddie's answer, whatever it may be, but seeing that suitcase had driven a new fear into the forefront of his mind – he couldn't help it. Maddie looked at the ground, her chest shuddering as she breathed in.

"I'm going away with the church."

"Today?"

"Mmhmm." She nodded.

"Why didn't you tell me before now?" His lower lip trembled as a realisation that he didn't want to acknowledge tried to force him to ask the more direct question. He willed her to just look at him and smile, like she usually did – or at least the way she always used to. Now that he thought about it, he hadn't seen a sincere, joyful smile on her face for a while. She glanced up at him for only a second, her eyes full of tears. *No*, he thought. *No no no...*

"D'ya know what? Doesn't matter. Works out better that you're already packed. Just give me five to throw some of my stuff in a bag and..."

"Billy."

"I'll come with you. We can go to the church thing."

"Billy, I'm sorry but..."

"Please don't say what I think you're going to say."

"I need to go. Even after all the therapy and everything, I was afraid you were still obsessing over all this stuff. I don't know how to help – you're not even trying to help yourself."

"I don't need drugs and therapy!"

"You think our neighbour is literally a monster." The last word came out choked but she managed not to break and cry.

"Reptilian." He couldn't resist the urge to correct her, and immediately wished he hadn't because she was shaking her head and walking towards him, or rather, past him. He almost moved to block her path but knew that forcing her to stand in the living room wouldn't do him any favours.

"Maddie, look, let's just go away together. Where's this church thing?"

"Wales," she mumbled. Oh god, she was taking her coat off the hook by the door.

"Great, we can look at that hotel you liked. Remember, the one you said would be a nice wedding venue?" His voice had taken on a pathetic, reedy tone, but he didn't care. Maddie scoffed at that – it was maybe only the second or third time in their six years that he'd heard her make such a scornful sound.

"You haven't cared about wedding venues for at least a year. Not since you started going on about stupid lizards and God knows what else." It wasn't just scorn, but bitter resentment. It took everything in him not to burst into tears, drop to his knees, and beg her to stay. She was right; since he'd learned the truth, he hadn't concerned himself with their engagement at all. Everything else that had once seemed important had paled into frivolity. He'd locked himself away with his laptop and made excuses every time she made an appointment to view a potential venue, or tried to ask him about cake flavours, or anything else regarding the planning of their wedding.

"I thought if I just went on this trip and we got some space, maybe the distance would... oh, I don't know." Maddie was pulling her coat on. Her voice was almost as small as her stature now. "But then you come in and say that about Mr. Tiley. You're not getting better."

"I don't need to get better!" he shouted, and found himself regretting his reflex response for the second time in a minute. She righted her toppled suitcase and gripped the handle. "Please," he was begging now. "I just need you to believe me."

"I can't." She took the set of keys that were hanging from the lock – her set with her car keys.

"Why? We've known each other since primary school. You *know me*, Maddie. Why can't you believe what I'm telling you I saw with my own eyes?"

"Because it's insane."

She opened the door and rushed outside, pulling her suitcase along on its wheels behind her, creating a physical barrier between them that took her out of his reach even as he followed her out onto the street.

She walked to her car, Billy trailing behind, openly weeping now, all sense of pride replaced with grief. He knew that there was only one set of things he could say to stop her; he was ill, he knew there were no reptilians controlling them, he would go back to his therapist, he would resume taking his medication.

But all of that was a lie.

She opened the boot of her car and put her suitcase inside, and then walked around to the driver's side door. As her fingers gripped the handle, she looked back at him, the sadness in her tear-filled eyes unbearable to look back at. He decided then that, for the first time ever, he was prepared to tell her an outright lie. He'd say whatever it took to stop her driving off, and he knew her well enough to know that's what she wanted. She never hesitated when she was absolutely set on a decision, but here she was, hesitating. Hoping.

He'd say what she wanted to hear, they'd make up, and then he'd suggest a romantic trip away to patch things up, so he could get them both out of the firing line and figure out his next move. He'd lay off the so-called conspiracy talk for a while, but slowly try to show her the truth. He'd work it in, try to get her to see.

"I don't suppose you've got my parcels, have you?"

The voice came from behind Billy. It sounded the same as it always had – light and friendly and with the gravel of old age and years of smoking – but it was enough to propel Billy forwards. He didn't turn to look at old Mr. Tiley as he fled back towards the safety of his house, and he didn't even look back over his shoulder at the love of his life as he widened the gap between them, cementing her decision to never close it again.

"I'm sorry, he's not feeling well," he heard Maddie tell the abomination that had the gall to hover in the street like he belonged there. It wasn't fair, but he hated her in that moment for not only *not* having his back, but for apologising for him like he was overreacting.

He slammed the door behind him for the second time that day.

It took him approximately five seconds to feel the complete and utter shame of abandoning Maddie in the process of literally running away. He hadn't even considered grabbing her first, or shielding her, or doing anything to protect her at all.

He took a breath, opened the door again and went back outside. But it was too late. Maddie was already in the car and pulling out of her parking space.

"No, Maddie!" he yelled, waving his arms. But she didn't stop, she left, and in the place where he'd last seen her standing, hoping he would change her mind, was Mr. Tiley.

"Everything alright, William?" the duplicitous snake asked, as if nothing was amiss. "She seemed quite upset."

"Are you fucking kidding me?" Billy spat, surprised to have found his voice, and laced with such vitriol. Perhaps he did have some gumption after all.

"Beg your pardon?" Mr. Tiley's wrinkled face crumpled further into a frown of broken, sun-spotted leather. He stood there in his thick, brown cardigan and flat cap, looking bewildered. He took a short, unsteady step forward, so Billy took one backwards. "What's the matter with you?"

"What's the...?" Billy spluttered. Tiley inched forward again and in response Billy thrust out both hands, palms out.

"Stop right there! I swear, if you come near me..." If he had time to think, Billy would have put a definitive threat at the end of the last sentence.

"Okay," Tiley replied in his softest, most soothing, I'm-just-a-nice-old-man voice. He stopped and held up his own palms. "Everything's alright, William. Is there someone I can call for you?"

"Call?"

"Madison said she'd call Tom to come over, but I think maybe I should call your mum?"

Now it wasn't just Tiley that looked bewildered: this interaction was outright bizarre to Billy. He'd seen Tiley – or rather, whatever it was that was posing as him – in his bedroom. Billy wasn't sure on the way that worked: if they killed and took the place of a human, or if they created the human suits they wore themselves – the Internet didn't have a conclusive verdict on that yet. He didn't know which reality was worse because he'd known Tiley since he was twelve. Hell, the guy – or whatever it was – used to babysit him. Regardless, Billy had seen him in his true form, his eighty-something year-old man suit crumpled naked on the floor like an outfit that had been shrugged off. It had lain strewn beneath the figure of gore that clung to the ceiling basking in the immense heat of a bedroom that was fitted with a dozen heat lamps. There were no scales on the body, as such, more like a fresh, raw layer of skin. It had made Billy feel sick, the way that slimy new flesh had pulsed like a heartbeat. And Tiley knew Billy had seen. He had chased him, for crying out loud. And now here he was, his wrinkled fingers fiddling with the hem of his cardigan, swaying from side to side like the doddering old man he always pretended to be, feigning concern, but for whose benefit?

Billy looked him up and down for the hundredth time, realising that those wrinkled old fingers did *look* the same as always, however. As did the rest of him. Deep lines were still etched into the man's sun-spotted forehead, and the space beneath both eyes was still littered with the same subtle but numerous creases, most likely caused from years of smiling and laughter. He looked the same as he always had. For a split second, Billy felt the doubt that Maddie must have. Looking at the guy, there was no way a reasonable person could believe that only minutes before, this guy had shed his flesh. Still, Billy knew what he had seen. Being off the medication he'd never wanted to take in the first place had nothing to do with it.

Did he put the skin suit back on? Or did he regenerate his appearance by will? Billy wondered. Tiley met Billy's glare with a bemused stare and took a step forward. Billy adjusted accordingly.

"I don't know what you think you're doing, but you don't want to come near me again, Tiley, or whatever your real name is," he spat. He was gearing himself up to make a full-on threat, but didn't know what would hurt or even scare a reptilian in a people suit. Plus, he'd never thrown a single punch in his life, let alone been a real danger to anyone.

"Am I nuts or are you two about to throw down?" It was Tom, and he was shooting them both quizzical looks as he strolled towards them. The relief that washed over Billy was immense. Tom was a head shorter than Billy and almost as slight in stature as Maddie, but he was back up, or at the very least, a witness should Tiley do something.

"Thomas, thank God you're here!" Tiley turned to him, his brown eyes wide with alarm. "I don't think he's well."

"I know, Maddie called me." Tom extended his arm and gave Tiley a pat on the shoulder, squeezing it for good measure before he let go. "Go on inside, mate. I'll take it from here."

"Are you sure? Should I call Lucy?"

"You stay away from my mum!" Billy all but screamed, his fists clenching at his sides. Tom looked from his friend to the old man, and replied with the slightest shake of his head and a wink.

"Nah, I'll calm him down. No worries."

"Stop talking about me like I'm not here, like I'm a deranged kid." Billy finally took his eyes away from Tiley and fixed Tom with his gaze instead. Tom stared back at him for a moment and then motioned to Tiley with his head that he should get going. Tiley cast one last, convincingly sincere glance at Billy, and then started shuffling off back towards his own house.

"Come on, mate, let's get you inside," Tom said, placing the same hand that he'd touched Tiley with on Billy's back. Billy started to protest, unwilling to turn his back on Tiley until he was gone, but Tom planted his other hand on Billy and steered him towards his own house. Billy flinched: the carpet graze from Tiley's stairs was rearing its ugly, stinging head, and Tom's hands had made him aware of it.

Inside, Tom went straight through to the kitchen and put the kettle on. Billy trailed behind him. His breathing had slowed some, but he was still soaking with continuous sweat.

He glanced around the living room, which now felt unbearably empty without Maddie in it. For the first time in a while, he noticed how badly the carpet needed to be vacuumed, and the ring marks on Maddie's one-of-a-kind coffee table, despite the stack of coasters on it that she'd begged him to use a thousand times. Tin foil ashtrays littered the place, along with empty Pepsi bottles and take-away wrappers. The place, he realised, was a shit hole, and no wonder. Maddie worked forty hours a week and dedicated half her spare time to her church, and despite losing his job because of his absences, Billy hadn't bothered to keep on top of things. He'd been more concerned with his research.

"Don't take offence but you look like shit," Tom said, busying himself with trying to find two clean mugs in the clutter of all the dirty ones crowded around on the work tops. He'd already checked the cupboard that housed them and found it empty.

"Oh no, why would I be offended at that?" Billy replied, but wasn't able to muster his usual level of sarcasm. "They're not just here, Tom. Tiley's one of them."

"Yeah, Maddie said you think Tiley's a lizard alien."

"Reptilian. I saw him, man, without his human skin on." Tom froze at the sink, with a sponge that had seen better days in one hand and a mug in the other. As he waited for the appropriate response, Billy absent-mindedly reached behind him and touched his lower back.

He winced. It took him a moment to remember how he'd managed to graze it so horribly. The skin of his back felt raw and angry. He pulled his hand away. The texture of the graze conjured the image of Tiley, raw on his ceiling.

"I knew I should never have bought you that bearded dragon." Tom finally said, and then went on washing the mugs.

"Really? You're making jokes at a time like this?"

"Spyro was cute as shit but obviously having a pet lizard snapped something in your head. I blame myself."

"Will you listen to me? They're here and not just here on Earth, but *here*." Billy gestured around as if 'they' were standing in his kitchen.

"Right. Well, that's put that on the back burner for now, shall we, and talk about—"

"Put it on the fucking back burner?"

"—And talk about what's really bothering you?" Tom interrupted, raising his voice to drown Billy out.

"What's bothering me is that the reptilian's are real, Tiley's one of them, and if he's here right across the goddamn street that means there are probably more."

"Okay. Or you're upset because Maddie finally had enough of this shit and left, and now you're spinning this yarn as a distraction? She said you stopped taking your meds. Do you find these – what are they called, delusions? – comforting or something?"

"What could possibly be comforting about the imminent fall of mankind?"

"I don't know!" Tom whirled around, the soapy mug slipping from his grasp as he did so and smashing as it landed by Billy's feet. "Whoops. I don't know, *William*. I'm not a psychiatrist. Do you want to talk about it?"

"I'm trying to talk about it!"

"About Maddie." Despite the all-encompassing major event on Billy's mind, the sound of her name hurt every time Tom said it. In comparison, he supposed that his girlfriend – fiancé – leaving him should have been but a mere scratch, but it wasn't. It was a large, gaping wound that was widening with every mention of her. Billy didn't respond to Tom's question, firstly because he didn't want to cry, and secondly because everyone's complete avoidance of the bigger problem at hand was infuriating.

"You should call her, try to get her back. That girl is a saint, mate."

"Tom, I saw this with my own eyes."

"I'm amazed she put up with this insanity for as long as she did, but if you'd just go back on your meds, talk to your doctor..."

"Tom, I saw it. He'd shed his skin and he was on the fucking ceiling."

"Jesus Christ, man. Do you hear yourself?"

"Trust me, I know it sounds mad, but I saw it."

"It's hard to trust you because yeah, you do sound mad."

"I can prove it."

"Oh God." Tom turned from the sink again, drying a mug that had a xenomorph printed on the side, a Christmas present that he had bought for Billy just last year. "What are you gonna do, stalk the guy with a hidden camera?"

"No need. I took a video." And with that statement, something in Tom's face finally changed.

"What do you mean?"

"I already had my phone in my hand because I was about to call an ambulance or the police or whatever. There was no answer when I went in so I thought he'd died. I think he was sleeping, I don't know," Billy shrugged, surprised that it was still his reflex to make so casual a gesture. "I filmed him, and then he woke up." There were a few seconds of silence and then Tom put down the mug and towel.

"Can I see?"

"Obviously." Billy drew his phone from his pocket and unlocked his screen. Tom closed the gap between them and stood at his side, peering down at the phone screen. Billy shuddered next to him as he got the video up and played it.

"Well." Tom took a deep breath in, let it out slowly. "Shit."

"You see the human suit there?" Billy pointed.

"Mmhmm."

"And Tiley there, on the..."

"Yeah, I see it."

"You believe me now?"

"Have to." Billy's lower lip trembled as relief flooded him. Finally.

"What are you gonna do with this?"

"Already sent it to my mum, and some of the guys from the groups."

"What groups?"

"Forums on the net."

"Ah."

"I'm thinking news outlets next, everywhere I can post it online, what do you think?"

"I think..." Tom hesitated, mulling over his responses. Billy waited, not quite smiling, but much happier than he had been two minutes before. "I think this sucks balls. You shouldn't have sent them to your mum."

"Why?"

"Because just you alone wouldn't have looked suspicious."

"Just me? What are you...?" Billy couldn't finish the sentence, because Tom hit him. He stumbled sideways in a drunken crabwalk, and then went down on his right hip. He gazed up at Tom from his kitchen floor, his left hand going to his cheek, which already throbbed something fierce. He was sure that had Tom caught him a little lower, his jaw would be broken, or at least a few teeth would have been loosened. The force of Tom's punch made no sense. Tom smiled down at him, flexing the offending hand, stretching the fingers out and wiggling them as if he were fitting them into a glove.

"I always wondered what that would be like."

"Wha...?" Billy climbed to his feet, backing away. His hip burned where he'd landed on it, and there was a pain shooting down from it to his knee, but he managed to right himself. Billy looked back into the eyes of the guy he'd considered his best friend for thirty years and tried to push back the same feeling he'd had just ten minutes before in the humid house across the road.

"I didn't want to do it here, but at least I won the pool," Tom said, his voice light and conversational. Billy just shook his head, lost for the words to form an appropriate response. "Tiley thought it would be another decade or so before you got any hard proof, but since you've already sent that stupid video to too many people, I guess the jig is up. I bet him we'd get to burn it all down before this year was up – that's what I was hoping for anyway."

"No," was all Billy managed.

"Yes!" Tom hissed, rubbing his hands together. "Exciting times! Your world is a cesspit, Billy boy. It's time for it to go." But before Tom had even finished gloating, Billy had fled the room.

Denial was very much where his mind was stubbornly trying to cling, but he'd read and seen enough online to know that once one of *them* started in on you, you ran. If this somehow turned out to be some inexplicable mistake, some really weird joke, then he could feel stupid about it and let Tom laugh about it later. But, his heart told him as he lurched through his living room, he was about to die.

Tom's footsteps thudded across the carpet behind him, then he heard them pounding across the wall instead. Hearing the sound of human feet sprinting across a wall was a mind-fraying experience that he could have done without hearing even once, at Tiley's house, never mind for a second time in the sanctity of his own home. Any real conscious thought was being screamed over by his instinct to escape, but somewhere dark in the back of his mind, it occurred to him that his home had never been a sanctuary anyway, because he'd always invited Tom into it. He'd told him everything, absolutely everything. Every detail of his own life, all his struggles with Maddie once the arguments started, and every discovery he made about the reptilians. Tom had never been his friend; he'd been his monitor.

Tom's footsteps went up the wall behind him, and in his peripheral vision he could see Tom's leering face as his gaze bore down on him, upside-down, from the ceiling. Tom was much faster and could have already caught him ten times over, but clearly that was the point he was making, and was trying to scare him. It did.

Billy, for the second time that day, burst into machine-gun sobs. His chest swelled with the pain of not having enough oxygen to expel the emotion or the sound, and he prayed that Tom's arrogance and insistence on taunting him would buy him enough time to get to the front door. If he could only make it outside, he had a chance.

The door crashed open, the door handle smashing into the wall as Tiley stepped into the house and rounded the corner into the living room. Billy almost skidded to a stop and started to turn, but Tom dropped down behind him, blocking his path.

"Tell me we can just start?" Tom asked Tiley.

"That's the word," Tiley replied, grinning. "Hallelujah!"

"Hallelujah!" Tom repeated, and then all but collapsed in the most unpleasant and vicious laughter Billy had ever heard. Billy couldn't tear his eyes from Tiley, who now looked a foot taller because he'd abandoned his previous eighty-something year-old posture. He stood tall and strong.

"We were going to carry on living amongst you, whispering nasty little nothings in your ears for a while longer, but thanks to you exposing us, there's no point," Tiley told Billy, beaming. His smile was just a little too wide. Tiny little tears in the skin at the corners of his mouth were appearing. Billy was still sobbing, his breath coming out in choked gasps.

"No one will believe me!" He hated that he was pleading, but what else was there? What did he think would happen by exposing them? He was not only helpless, by his own rendering, but stupid. "They'll think the video is fake!"

"It's already being shared across the pond," Tom replied, his eyes closing for a second.

"You can't know that!" Billy almost shouted. The desperation in his voice made him cringe.

"We do know that." Tiley grinned and tapped the side of his head.

"No," Billy exhaled.

"Yes!" Tiley and Tom shrieked in unison. Something passed silently between them after that. As Billy watched the wordless exchange in helpless horror, the sickening comprehension of what he was actually witnessing dawned on him.

Hivemind.

Then there were teeth in the back of Billy's neck – not the tearing, reptilian fangs he might have expected, but plain old human teeth. They hurt plenty. He'd barely time to struggle before Tom wound his arms around his torso, pinning his own arms to his side. Tom – *it* – chewed his flesh. A warmth grew in Billy's stomach and the room started to tilt – it was the same feeling he'd had when he'd donated blood once. It was a strangely pleasant feeling and a deceptive one, because it marked one giant step towards fainting.

For all his contingency plans, the weapons stashed around his house, and all the talk he had given both Maddie and Tom (and didn't he feel foolish about *that* now?) about how he'd fight when the day came, he found himself paralysed. The shame of being so utterly held by fear started to drown him in the darkness that was creeping in.

Billy's last thought was that he hoped Maddie was already far away and that she'd never come back.

And then, he was gone.

THE END

Just Like Baking

Everyone avoided the very end of Willow Street because there dwelled Thistle Cottage. It set itself apart as the only detached home in the area, that fact alone giving it an air of superiority over its terraced neighbours. A low bungalow, with actual thatch still lacing its roof, it was a miracle the ivy-covered stone was still standing. A miracle, or a curse, many whispered. It looked as new as the day it was built.

It was especially given a wide berth on a night like tonight – blacker than the devil's eyes, with rain lashing down on those foolish enough to get caught in the downpour. Thunder boomed overhead and shook the very foundations in which those below cowered. Forked lightning stabbed at the sky, backlighting thick clouds that peered down on the earth like twisted faces. Wind whistled and whipped at fence posts. It pulled lovingly planted flowers from their beds in the gardens of Willow Street, yanking every bit of cheerful colour away and tossing the severed petals into the storm.

And yet, black hood pulled tight around her head, her black garments billowing out behind her as though the Dark Lord himself were blowing her a kiss, *she* approached Thistle Cottage. She with no fear.

Inside the cottage, they had gathered.

Four of them, their eyes closed, hands joined together in a circle, sat at the table in the living room, each one at a corner. One hundred candles illuminated the room, their flickering flames casting shadows that danced. Incense and oils burned. The only sound was the storm raging outside; the air inside the dwelling humming with power.

Linked, they were channelling energy, preparing for their most dangerous and daring incantation. Contrary to the gossip, they could not control the elements. However, in order to cast this particular spell, they had to wait for the perfect conditions: thunder, lightning, wind, and rain. It could be harnessed only if the deepest concentration could be achieved.

The energy between them buzzed, raising the fine hairs on the back of their arms and their necks. It was working, it was...

All of their eyes snapped open at the sound. North, South, and West glared at East. It took her a second and then swearing, she fumbled in her pocket.

"Goddamnit, East!" North complained.

"Sorry, I thought I'd put it on silent," East muttered, her cheeks blazing like the sun. "Hello, Mum?"

"And she's answering it!" West complained, letting go of the hands either side of her to throw hers up in the air in a gesture of annoyance. She pushed back her velvet hood, revealing long hair the colour of spun gold.

"I told you not to call until after nine, we're trying to summon... no! Oh, Mu-uuum! That's not fair!" East raised her eyes to each of her group for help, but of course they could only hear her side of the conversation and had no idea what exactly she expected from them. "I'm not a kid anymore, I shouldn't have to... It is *not* my fault she has no friends! She's not the easiest person to... but it's summoning night! Why can't she join yours instead?" East shoved herself back from the table and left the room, arguing with her mother about how there was simply no room at the inn.

North, South, and West glanced around at each other, sighing. Not their real names of course, but one always uses an alias when summoning any force, in case of a lurking, listening intruder.

"What's that all about then, you reckon?" South wondered. The others shrugged.

"I'm getting snacks," West declared, getting up from the table.

"Okay but eat them in the kitchen. We can't risk getting crumbs in here," North reminded her. West nodded but rolled her eyes. She wasn't stupid.

"East better get her ass back in here before the rain stops and we lose our chance." South drummed her fingers on the burgundy velvet tablecloth. West paused on her way to the door to look out of the window. She pulled the heavy curtain aside and peered out into the dark.

"Don't worry, it's still coming down by the bucket-load out... oh, shit."

"What?" North and South turned with comical synchronisation.

"It's her little sister."

"Guys, I'm so sorry!" East burst back into the room, enraged. "My stupid mum said I have to let her join in. She's upset, apparently."

"Why?" South had always been the most tolerant and compassionate.

"Her own coven is ghosting her again," East sighed.

"But there are already four of us!" North protested, knowing it was pointless.

"Mum said we can still do it with five if we're extra careful. That little dickhead told her I'd already agreed."

"You told your sister she could join us tonight?" West was rolling her eyes again.

"Of course not, she lied. What a shock." Before East could apologise or lament further about the injustices of being the older sister, the dreaded knock on the door came. "Fucking ridiculous still being made to let my stupid little sister tag along," she grumbled on her way to the door. "I'm two-hundred-and-seventeen, for God's sake."

The other three, now all back in their seats, cemented themselves to them so that they couldn't be ousted. Everyone – especially East's powerful, nurturing mother – knew that the most effective covens were made up of four, not five.

"It's really coming down out there!" Abbie declared, from the entryway. They listened, hoping against all rational hope that East would just boot her sister back out into the downpour.

"What the fuck are you wearing?" came East's grumbling reply.

"What? Mum said to wear black." Abbie banged open the living room door and entered, casting an enthusiastic smile at everyone, while a disgruntled East trailed behind, looking her up and down from the back. She pulled back the hood of her coat – an enormous puffer-style effort that reached her knees, with an oversized rounded hood that somewhat resembled an astronaut's helmet. The entire garment looked like a load of inflatables stitched together – it was a wonder she'd merely been drenched instead of blown away.

"Hey guys, what's going down in funky town?" she breathed, her eyes glistening with excitement as they swept over the crystals, candles, and trinkets, each of which were placed carefully and deliberately around the room. She shrugged off her coat and made to drape it on the back of North's chair, dripping remnants of the storm into a pool right where the wood met North's butt. Irritated, she shuffled forward. East gathered up the ridiculous thing and left the room to hang it elsewhere.

"Interesting... er... tights," South offered, forcing a smile for their unwanted company. At one-hundred-and-ninety-two, she was the closest to Abbie's age (though still almost a century older), and therefore felt obligated to be friendly whenever she was buzzing around. A bolt of distrust shot across Abbie's forehead for a second, lining the space between her eyebrows like someone had scored the flesh, and then her face softened and she looked down at her legs, smiling. She was clad in black tights decorated with silvery cobwebs and spiders – courtesy of her favourite clothing store, Blue Banana. Above them, she wore a pink and black tutu, and a fishnet shirt with the shoulders cut out, on top of a white shirt and a black tie. At her feet were black ballet pumps with cat faces on the toes – quite possibly the most weather inappropriate shoes (besides sandals or slippers) that she could have picked. Rounding off the look was the backpack dangling from the crook of her elbow, dripping onto the carpet. It was Yoda.

The rest of them, by contrast, wore understated long black dresses beneath heavy, velvet cloaks.

"You look like you rolled blind drunk through a goth charity shop," East told her through black lipsticked lips, re-entering the room.

"You look like the Wish version of Morticia Addams," Abbie retorted.

"You look like Avril Lavigne cosplaying as a Tim Burton character."

"Well, at least I don't take my makeup tips from *The Crow*."

"You haven't even fucking seen *The Crow*!" The makeup remark, combined with Abbie's actual lack of pop culture knowledge, actually annoyed her. "You're an idiot."

"Yeah? Well, you're a cunt."

"Come on now, ladies," South interjected. "Little Bird, I probably would have dressed just like you at your age, if clothes like that had existed back then. We just had to make do." Abbie smiled at her in gratitude, and then tipped her head at East with her eyebrows raised in a 'haha I won' expression, which wasn't South's intention, but if these two started like they usually did, they'd never get to the summoning.

"Take a seat, we can still do it with five," North said, patting the table next to her, where East went. Abbie went for the chair, but East yanked her back by the shoulder.

"Not in my seat. I'll get the foldout chair," she said, with a knowing smirk.

"Why do I always have to sit on the foldout chair?" Abbie complained.

"Because you're the youngest and that's the order of things," East replied, and then disappeared from the room. A silence passed.

"Foldout chairs are bullshit," Abbie sulked.

"Little Bird, have you participated in a summoning before?" North asked her. Abbie nodded. "A binding?" Abbie hesitated, and then shook her head. The three sucked in breaths simultaneously. "Okay," North proceeded, shaking her head. "The most important thing is for us all to be in sync with each other. We've done this a few times, always successfully, but there's a lot of margin for error. Every detail, every *thought* has to be right, or else the thing might end up freeing itself of us."

"And that would be bad," South added.

"Yeah," North agreed. "Very bad." They looked at what they all secretly regarded as the intruder, waiting for confirmation that she understood the seriousness of the situation. Her eyes were glazed over, and she was staring off towards her sister's bookcase, not really seeing the ancient, leather and flesh-bound books, but whatever little fantasy had sprung up in her mind and lifted her out of the conversation.

"Little Bird!" It was West this time.

"Hmm?"

"Are you listening?"

"Yeah. Spell, demon, spooky. Got it."

"This is serious, if you..."

"What's in the stupid bag?" East interrupted, returning with an extra chair. She handed it to Abbie to unfold and took her own seat.

"Oh, I made muffins!" Abbie beamed. She unfolded her chair, dropped Yoda on to it, and then reached in and produced the efforts she claimed were muffins, still housed in their clingfilmed baking tray. She tore away the film and dropped the tray onto the table, disturbing the crystals, cards, entwined herbs and flowers, and one of the pillar candles, which she tipped over, spilling wax out onto the burgundy cloth.

"Goddamnit!" East complained, righting the candle and immediately going at the wax, lest it ruin her favourite cloth. Abbie ignored her and gestured to the tray.

"Go on then, try them! I made them especially."

"Where are they?" South asked, sincerely perplexed, staring at the cupcake tray that was devoid of muffins. All she could see were sticky, crispy imitations of sponge stuck to the bottom of each well – the remains of muffins that had been scraped out, probably because, from the look of it, Abbie had neglected to use any cupcake holders to bake them in. South wondered how anyone could possibly just pour muffin mix straight into the tray without realising it was wrong.

"There," Abbie pointed, now also perplexed.

"Oh!" South nodded, realising that the glued in, flat-as-pancake leftovers were indeed the actual muffins. "Did you...?"

"What the hell? Did you use self-raising flour or baking soda or anything?" East poked at the tray. Abbie slapped her hand away.

"Yes." She was irritated. "I'm not an idiot."

"Did you weigh out the ingredients, hon'?" South was always externally kinder than East, but internally rolled her eyes more than the rest of them combined.

"Nah, just chucked it all in a bowl. Baking's not an exact science, is it."

"I mean, it is..." East argued, her chest hitching with laughter. Before Abbie could get angry and another argument could ensue, North plucked the tray off the table and handed it to the master baker.

"We'll save them for after, as a treat," she said, always the expert at placation. "We really need to get on with the summoning while we still have the storm. Why don't you put these in the kitchen and bring back the daffodils?" Abbie took the tray but stayed where she was. There was a beat. "They're dehydrated, crushed daffodils, in a little jar, on the worktop by the sink."

"Okay!" Abbie left the room. Everyone breathed out a sigh.

"I'm gonna kill my mum," East grumbled.

"Good luck with that. She's immortal," West smiled. "But for real, should we cancel?"

"No way," North insisted. Our local farms are struggling – have you seen the price of eggs recently?"

"If you can even get them," South interjected.

"Yeah," North agreed. "We haven't seen a tomato in weeks. The soil's barren. Our local council has turned to the Dark Side..."

"I'm surprised they haven't started whinging about disrespect, and killing the younglings," South smirked, staring at Abbie's Yoda backpack.

"Our roads are full of potholes," North continued. "The weather is always horrible, all the local businesses are going bust so redundancy is off the charts, and no one around here has even won so much as a pound on a scratch card in years. Not to mention all the crap that's happening everywhere else. Did you hear about that guy they found eaten to death in his own house the other day?"

"We get the point." West rolled her eyes but was smiling. "She's joined us before and nothing's gone wrong, I suppose."

"This town needs some good fortune, and we're the ones that can give it," North finished. She drummed her fingers on the table and turned her head towards the door. "What is taking that girl so long?"

"Okay, but just a reminder that I'm against binding a demon to do our charitable bidding for the sake of the dickholes around here," West half-joked. "They'd be chasing us with pitchforks, if this were the old days."

"You shouldn't joke about pitchforks," East mumbled, her eyes glazing over a little. "The prongs really hurt." She gazed inward at some unpleasant memory, and absent-mindedly rubbed her thigh.

"It's not their fault," North shrugged. "People have always been afraid of us, especially since they sense we're different but don't know why. We can help, so we should."

"You're so full of shit, North," South chuckled. "Get off your high horse. This is just because you're dying for an omelette."

"Well, what am I meant to eat? I can't have carbs, I'm on keto!" North cried, completely serious.

"Okay, let's do this!" Abbie declared, returning with a small jar of yellow dust in hand. She shoved Yoda to the floor and took his place. "Leeroy Jenkins!" She looked around, grinning. Everyone stared back, with no clue as to the reference.

"Let's just start," East sighed. "Ladies, join hands."

And then there were five.

Eyes closed, they breathed deeply in unison. Establishing the connection between them and ensuring their bond held them fast was crucial before opening any spiritual doors. At first, it was just about coordination; then, only when all members were entirely focused on a single, shared goal, it would become an active and unbreakable psychic link. An impenetrable, locked, *safe* environment, which no outside force – conjured or otherwise – could manipulate. A simple summoning was easy enough – teenagers around the world, many even without the natural gift of the craft – did it accidentally all the time. North often commented that whoever had commercialised Ouija Boards was both a marketing genius, and most likely a disgruntled, society-hating witch without a coven to keep her straight. Anyone could perform a summoning. But a binding, that was another matter. Only a powerful, loyal coven could bind itself to a demon without risking dire consequences.

Abbie wasn't formally a member, of course, but she was a natural witch and an immediate blood relative of the head of the coven. Plus, this wasn't her first time with them.

Their lips moved quickly in unison, inaudible devotions of purity and love, praying to nature to guide them in their bid to make the following days just that little bit brighter for their neighbours.

Abbie cracked one eye open, repressing a giggle. Her sister and friends were so old-school with their magic. And they looked funny in their robes. The stuff of Hollywood witch stereotypes. She was surprised they weren't blasting a Stevie Nicks CD – or a vinyl – to accompany their outdated but admittedly effective incantation.

"Okay, I think that's good," East said eventually. She let go of the hands either side of her and rose to her feet. Abbie and West joined hands behind East's back, re-forming the circle and enclosing East safely within it. As if conscious and awakening in preparation, the cauldron in the centre of the table began to glow. She picked up a crystal and one of the dried herb bundles and dropped them inside. "Incinerate," she whispered, and thick smoke spilled out of the cauldron's mouth.

"Which demon are we summoning?" Abbie whispered to North.

"Any that is foolish enough to get involved," North whispered back. "It doesn't matter – they're everywhere all the time. Now shush and focus." Abbie didn't let go of the hands she was holding, but glanced around the room, suddenly nervous.

"Are there any in here now?"

"Many. You'll be able to sense them as you mature and your power develops. Now, be quiet." North closed her eyes again, trying to centre herself with East's voice as she whispered invocations and dropped ingredients into the cauldron. The room, despite all the candles, was somehow growing darker.

"But why are they already here?" Abbie persisted. North took in a breath, determined to remain composed, because the last thing you wanted to add to a spell that summoned a demon was anger.

"Because witches are more of a challenge to possess than regular people, and they're dickholes that want to one-up us. Now please, concentrate."

East tipped the crushed daffodils, the last of the ingredients, into the cauldron and then lowered her face to it, blowing gently into the smoke. For just the slightest, almost inconceivable moment, the smoke stared back at her, the glow of red eyes flickering and disappearing in the mist. East jolted backwards, almost breaking the hold that Abbie and West had on each other.

"What's wrong?" West looked up.

"I don't... did you see...?" East was shaking her head.

"I saw it," South whispered, the colour draining from her face. "But we did everything the same: the same ingredients, the same process, the same measurements?" The creeping darkness in the room was closing in from the corners, its black emptiness spreading inward like molten tar.

"Yes, I'm certain, it was the same as always," East tried to reassure herself, even as she shivered. With the darkness came the ice. "I don't understand." As she waved her arms, a scent hit her. A scent from the small jar that had housed the daffodils, the jar she was still holding. She brought it to her nose and sniffed. "Oh my God. Little Bird, what is this?"

"The jar from the worktop by the fridge," Abbie replied, already defensive. North's head snapped towards her.

"What? I said the jar on the worktop by the *sink*."

"Oh." Abbie shrugged and bit her lower lip in an exaggerated comical expression of 'whoopsie' that no one – not even South, who often offered pity laughs – reacted to.

"Fucking hell, it's turmeric," East told them, taking another sniff. Whispering filled the room – the words they could not understand, but the malicious and gleeful intent was clear.

"What's going to happen?" Abbie dared ask, feeling responsible but not enough to yet apologise for whatever annoyance she may have caused.

"We've opened the door but now we can't bind what comes through," South told her, this time not bothering with the effort of sounding neutral, let alone kind.

"Can it possess us?!" Abbie squeaked, looking at each of them in turn. When no one answered, beginning to panic, she let go of West's hand so she could grip on to North.

"No, don't break the circle!" West screeched. Her lips were turning blue. Ice was forming and travelling along the walls like thick spider-web strands.

"Natalie, will it get me because I'm the youngest?" Abbie bleated, her fingers digging into North's arm now. North's eyes widened at the sound of her real name.

"No names! Goddamnit!" East yanked her sister backwards, turned her, and slapped her across the face. She wasn't really sure what the use was, but it was satisfying so she did it a second time.

"I'm sorry!" Abbie yelped, as her sister shook her by her shoulders. "I forgot!"

"How convenient for me." The voice came out of North's mouth, but it wasn't hers. The others turned towards her, their mouths falling open even wider than their eyes, which were now all saucers. The thing that had hijacked North grinned at them, her mouth splitting slightly at the corners as it forcibly overstretched her features.

"Double double, toil and trouble!" it screeched, then threw its head back laughing. East was reaching for the bowl of crushed herbs, her thoughts turning over a million at a time, trying to remember the exorcism failsafe that she had never had to use, but had learned from her mother in case of an emergency. But it didn't matter. North jumped to her feet, gave them all a double middle finger, and then turned and sprinted through the wall into the kitchen. Not through the door, through the wall. North's poor human body undoubtedly broke in several places in the process, but the thing inside her wouldn't feel that.

"Get her!" South screamed, coming to her senses. "We can't let her get out of the house!" All but Abbie were on their feet and running for the kitchen. She sat there, stunned, watching as South and West darted through the door, and for some reason, East squeezed through the lady-sized hole in the wall.

"Oh shit." South stopped in the kitchen doorway, holding her hands up in a peaceful gesture. "Don't do anything nuts," she begged.

North was grinning, holding the sweeping brush she had found propped up against the sink.

"Fly, my pretties!" it laughed. It found itself hilarious.

"No!" the rest of them screamed. Abbie appeared in the doorway, clutching a lit pillar candle. North peered at her through the gloom, a wry grin twisting just one side of her mouth.

"And what, pray tell, do you plan to do with that?" it enquired. Abbie lowered her eyes to the flame, whispered something so quickly it was inaudible, and then flung the tiny pool of melted wax from the head of the candle in North's direction, splattering her face with it. North still gripped the sweeping brush with one hand, but the other flew to her face and she started shrieking. For a split second, East dared feel hopeful and, for the first time ever, proud. Her little sister had memorised the banishment spell that she had been unable to conjure from memory in her stress, and though the success rate of that particular spell was low, they seemed to be in luck.

"I'm melting! Ahhhh! Melting!" North screeched, bending at the knee and wiggling her hips like a drunk belly dancer. The smile vanished from East's face. North cackled and then returned her hand to the sweeping brush. West dared edge closer, but the thing hijacking North noticed and swung a leg over the brush handle.

"Bored now." She grinned, levitated several feet into the air, and then went shooting through the closed kitchen window, shattering the glass and the immaculately preserved wooden window frame. They watched her zoom off into the night, her cackles taunting them even through the howling wind.

East, West, and even South all turned to glare at Abbie. She hung her head, not daring to look at them. East opened her mouth to berate her, and then a blinding flash of lightning illuminated the entire sky, and the whole kitchen, and all of them saw red. Literally.

"Oh no... is that...?" South turned, brushing past Abbie as she left the kitchen. They followed her silently out of the front door and on to the street, their faces turning up into the rain. Which was now blood.

East's phone rang. She turned back into the house, already dripping red, not caring about the original wooden floors because stains wouldn't matter for much longer now.

"Hi, Mum, what's up...? No, we knew what we were doing... well, to be honest, you shouldn't have sent her. Turmeric." She held the phone away from her ear for a moment while her mother screamed obscenities at her. "So, what does blood rain mean exactly? Uh-huh, hold on a sec." She covered the phone with her hand and addressed the group. "Apocalypse," she confirmed.

"Aw, goddamnit!" West responded, trudging back into the house. The others followed.

"How is it *my* fault?" East, back on the phone now. "But *you* made me include her!"

She moved off into the kitchen to continue her argument.

In the entryway, South and West just stared at Abbie, their faces completely smeared with blood, their arms folded. West's beautiful blonde hair was now the colour of a saturated tampon. On the roof above them, the sound of hammering blood rain gave way to something else, something heavier, more substantial. It sounded like thousands of pebbles raining down upon them. West glanced out of the open front door and groaned before turning her accusatory gaze back on Abbie.

It was also raining teeth.

THE END

Catch Fire

Emily sat holding her car keys in a clenched fist, looking down at her lap. Beside her, Matt sighed through his nose and crossed his arms over his chest. He still wore his seatbelt.

"It's not too late to just turn around and go home," he told her, his voice rising ever so slightly through the back half of his statement. Emily fixed a smile onto her face but didn't dare to look up at him yet.

"I just need a second before we go in, that's all," she said, forcing a lightness she didn't feel into her response. "It's been a while."

"Not long enough." Matt glared out of the passenger side window at his sister-in-law's house. Emily didn't know what to say without prompting yet another argument about accepting her sister's dinner invitation on their behalf, without consulting him first. She knew he would have said no.

A stony minute of silence passed between them, which was plenty of time for Emily to once again remind herself that she was weak and pathetic in her inability to just cut ties with the cause of most of her troubles.

Matt had been patient at first, but time and the many incidences he'd either witnessed or been drawn into had erased his capacity for giving 'just one more' second chance. Emily understood his perspective – agreed with it, in fact – but somehow just couldn't force herself into the same mindset.

She almost wished that Matt had refused to come. That way, at least she wouldn't have his judgment to contend with on top of whatever was coming for the rest of the evening. But Matt wasn't the kind of man that would send his unarmed wife into a snake pit. He was the kind of man that would sooner wrestle a snake with his bare hands than allow it to bite his wife, or failing that, at least be on hand with an anti-venom. He'd done it a hundred times in the five years they'd been together.

"You could have just stayed at home," Emily mumbled into her lap, feeling guilty. He turned his gaze towards her, dropped his arms from his chest, and surprised her by pulling one of her hands away from her keys and kissing it.

"And let you go in there on your own? No way." He half-smiled. "Look, I'm not mad at *you*. Sorry for being a dickhead."

"You're not?"

"Just frustrated. She was finally gone."

"I know."

"She ruined our wedding."

"She didn't *ruin* it."

"Turned up in a white dress, aired your sexual past during the speeches after we told her not to make one, pretended to faint as you were walking down the aisle..."

"Alright, alright." Emily felt heat rise in her face. The image of her sister "fainting" and slipping off her chair (but gently enough to avoid injury somehow, despite apparently being unconscious), right into the aisle as she tried to walk down it was forever seared into her wedding day memories. That day had been the final straw, but it was just the most recent in a long line of incidences over the years, in which Emily had ended up in floods of tears and dear sister Jen always somehow looked like either a victim or a martyr.

"Babe, for the life of me, I do not understand why you're interested in anything that bitch has to say. She just wants to worm her way back in."

"She wants to apologise properly," Emily said, wanting to believe her own words but not quite managing.

"She always does."

"She sounded really sincere on the phone."

"She. Always. Does."

"I think she means it this time, though." She looked at Matt and he sighed, his thumb circling the back of her hand.

"You always do." Another moment of silence in which Emily couldn't argue because he was absolutely right. "You're such a nice person, Em, and I love you for that, but I wish you could just accept that Jen will never change, and you're better off without her."

"She has..."

"Problems, I know. But that's not your fault, and you can't fix things for her."

"I know she's horrible to me sometimes and has to make everything about her, but I don't think she can help it. She's been through some really bad stuff."

"Has she?" Matt's eyebrows almost shot all the way up into his hairline. "Because at least half the crap she's called you crying about turned out to be a massive, elaborate lie to get money out of you, or get you to drive to her house at midnight over nothing. She's the master of making you feel guilty enough to do just about anything."

"I'm afraid to completely cut her off in case she..." Emily trailed off, staring into her lap again.

"She's not fragile like that, babe. She just wants you to think she is so she can use it as an excuse every time she does something shitty to you." He was right, of course. But he also just didn't understand. There was no way he could because he was an only child.

"I just want to hear her out. This is the last time and if *anything* seems off, I swear I'm done. Mum and Dad have been on my case about being the bigger person so Christmas isn't awkward. We won't stay long," Emily promised, pulling her hand out of his to free up the one holding the keys so she could open her door.

"Okay," Matt sighed. "Into the fray."

Out of the car and up the front path, they stood in front of Jen's looming house – twice the size of theirs – and braced themselves before knocking on the door. Matt had always questioned how Jen could afford such a nice place, considering that her employment status over the last two decades had been erratic at best. She'd been fired from more jobs than Matt and Emily had ever had combined. Emily knew how Jen afforded it but had never told Matt because she knew he'd question it, and she wanted to avoid an argument about whether or not Jen was a survivor or an outright liar in a situation that had resulted in a massive payoff.

"I bet she hasn't even started cooking yet," Matt muttered as Emily rang the bell.

As footsteps approached, Emily did her best to line her face with a 'I'll-hear-you-out-but-I-haven't-forgiven-you-yet' smile – the kind of smile that one gives to a passing stranger on the street after awkwardly making eye contact but not wanting to look hostile or impolite. The effort, however, was wasted because it wasn't Jen – the only person they were expecting to see tonight – that answered the door.

A man with tousled dark hair that matched neat facial hair greeted them. He wore an impeccably ironed blue shirt and black, pinstriped trousers that ended in what were clearly very expensive leather shoes. Besides his formal attire, he looked remarkably like Matt.

Emily, in a bid to be polite, tore her eyes away from his shoes before she was able to even hazard a guess at the brand, which was a waste of time anyway as designer brands were an alien concept to her. She couldn't help but wonder how a guy wearing real leather could be allowed in Jen's house after the absolute chaos that had ensued only last Christmas, when Emily had received an eyeshadow pallet from their mother that didn't turn out to be cruelty free – a fact that Emily wasn't even aware of it until Jen went out of her way to look it up. Jen had berated her over that pallet until Emily binned it.

"Let's see, gorgeous haircut... you must be Emily!" The man beamed, and then looked to Matt. "Which makes you Matt. Come in, come in, come in!" He turned and waltzed off through the foyer towards the kitchen, leaving them to close the door and follow him. Emily touched the left side of her head and smoothed the short hair down as she stepped inside. Matt took her hair-smoothing hand and kissed it. He knew what she was thinking: was this dude aware of why half of her hair was thick and hanging to her waist, while the other was severely short in comparison, growing out from being shaved? Was he taking the piss, or did he sincerely not know that Emily's 'undercut' was a result of Jen trying to buzzcut her entire head – apparently for a joke – during her hen party? That, as far as Matt was concerned, should have been the last straw, but Emily had been too afraid to cause family drama by disinviting her to their wedding.

"You look beautiful," he assured her, and though she didn't believe him, his compliment did serve to halt the rapid downward spiral of her self-esteem. She smiled at him, absolutely loving the man, because thanks to a complete and utter lack of a social filter, Matt never said anything he didn't sincerely mean.

"It looks like the Addams family redecorated in here," he whispered as they both looked around the foyer. The doors off to the left were all closed, and thanks to the burgundy walls, which were magnolia last time they had visited, the large space looked small and dark. The doorframes and banister had been coated with an almost black varnish. Incense sticks littered the small decorative tables, tendrils of sandalwood-scented smoke curling into the air around them. Emily, in a bid to not incentivise Matt to get irritated, repressed the urge to sigh. Jen was about a decade late in copying her, but this was almost exactly how Emily had decorated her bedroom in her first student house.

Matt made an exaggerated display of sniffing the air.

"Ooh, do you smell what's cooking?" he asked her, animating his nose like a cartoon character following a scent as they proceeded to the open door on the right, towards the kitchen.

"No?" Emily took a breath, concentrating. All she could get was the almost overwhelming smell of burning incense. "What is it?"

"Absolutely fuck all!" Matt stage whispered. She laughed, and into the kitchen they went.

There was, indeed, absolutely fuck all in the oven, though the oven light was on. *She's preheating it*, Emily thought, though she couldn't see a roasting dish anywhere. In fact, there were no signs of food out in the kitchen at all – cooked, chopped or even peeled. *Goddamnit*, she thought. Matt was right, and she'd be hearing about it later when they got home. He'd eaten a sandwich right before leaving the house despite the 7pm dinner invitation because historically speaking, Jen had not once ever served dinner anywhere near the time she'd stated, after insisting they turn up on time. Emily had (foolishly, she was disappointed but prepared to admit) taken Jen on her word and not eaten a thing since lunch.

That was Strike One, Emily decided, though if she were being honest, she didn't know if that meant anything because she'd never been able to bring herself to limit the amount of strikes Jen had to get before she gave up on her. Three. Tonight, it would be three, and then they were out.

Strike Two came immediately after, when Emily looked through the kitchen to the adjoining dining area to see Jen and the mysterious suited man, as well as another couple, sitting at the enormous dining table. During their phone call the week before, Jen had cried, begged, and emphatically insisted that she *needed* to see them, to speak with them alone, to make amends for her past behaviour. *I've been getting therapy*, she'd said. *I want to take accountability for my actions.* And yet, here she was, surrounded by a tiny but unmistakable army of friends, shielded. Emily internally scolded herself for being surprised because this was one of Jen's classic moves. There she was, laughing it up with what she presumed was her new boyfriend, basically a carbon copy of Matt, as if this were any other Saturday night.

Her husband's grip on her hand tightened a little as he bristled next to her, his thoughts mirroring hers, though it was more evident on his face.

"Evening, Jen." Emily was loud enough for the heads of the other guests to turn in her direction, but it took Jen a few more seconds to divert her attention from the guy who looked like Matt.

"Oh, Emily! Matt!" Jen squealed, as if she'd had no idea they were there. "I'm so happy you're here!" She all but slammed her half-empty wine glass down on the table in a show of haste to get to her feet, and then she was running from the head of the table towards them, arms flung wide, smile to match. She slammed into Emily and wrapped her arms around her. Emily, already beginning to broil inside, affixed a polite smile to her own face as she looked over her sister's shoulder to the other guests, who were all staring and smiling at Jen's back as if she were the most adorable thing they'd ever seen.

Jen then flung herself in Matt's direction and attempted to wrap him up the same way, but he shifted his body sideways so she was forced to lean into him at an angle, and he left his arms hanging at his sides. Emily's eyes went from him to the guests, whose expressions had turned south as they witnessed Matt's reaction, averting their eyes. The very specific stomach knot that Emily thought had finally dissolved forever came back, turning and twisting and fraying in her gut. She couldn't have eaten so it was just as well that the dinner part of the invitation was phony after all.

She shouldn't have cared about the opinions of her sister's group, but she did. One of Jen's specialties was to put Emily on the backfoot in a social setting and paint her as a bad person, all the while appearing to everyone else like she was doing the opposite: like the time Emily had, in confidence, told her that she'd suffered a miscarriage, and then not one hour later, Jen decided it was a good day to announce her own (fake) pregnancy, and then acted bewildered and confused when Emily lost her mind in front of their grandmother. She always came off looking like a loving, doting, sometimes innocently naïve host, whose family were quick to demonise her over misunderstandings.

These people had no idea why Emily and Matt were there, what had passed between them and Jen, or why Matt was too uncomfortable to hug her back. All they knew was what they saw:

Jen enthusiastically and excitedly expressing affection, her sister returning it with little interest, and her brother-in-law being outright rude.

Jen let go of Matt, stepped back, shot him a quizzical look, and then to everyone else said, "O-*kay*." She followed it up with a well-practiced light but awkward giggle and returned to her seat at the head of the table. "Sit, sit, sit!" she told them. *Come in, come in, come in*, Emily thought, with a stab of irritation. Jen's chameleonic tendency to emulate those around her had always annoyed her. She figured it was some sort of social reflex produced by low self-esteem, and felt bad that it bothered her so much if it was a coping mechanism. Regardless, Emily was unsettled by Jen's ability to slip out of one skin and into another so effortlessly, and bothered by the fact that no one else ever caught on. Not even she knew what Jen's true personality was anymore, and she doubted Jen did either.

They took their seats opposite the other couple.

This room was as dark as the foyer and decorated more intricately. Black floor-to-ceiling curtains were drawn across the sliding patio doors, obscuring what was usually a lovely view of the mountains, especially on nights like tonight when the sky was blanketed with stars. The kitchen area had been left alone, and almost looked odd with its cream, marbled worktops and cupboards. The dining area had been stripped of its gold wallpaper and was now painted black. There were strange symbols painted on the far wall behind Jen. They were clearly the work of a talented, steady hand, but they were unsettling all the same. Drawn on top of the black in silver, they gave the impression of carvings etched into the wall. The room was also thick with incense smoke, plumes of it seemed to be attacking them from all directions. The only thing missing were black candles. In fact, Emily was surprised to notice, there wasn't a single lit candle anywhere. It would certainly fit with the décor, and cast away some of the gloom.

"Emmy, this is my boyfriend, Joe," Jen said, gesturing towards the man who had let them in. "The Pastor introduced us." Emily had no idea who 'The Pastor' was, but she smiled and nodded anyway.

"Nice to meet you," Joe said, his smile matching Jen's. "I've heard so much about you guys." Emily wondered what exactly he'd heard and how much of it was skewed, or entirely fabricated. He continued to smile as he circled the table and took his seat at the end facing Jen.

"And you remember Beth and Toby?"

"Mmhmm. Nice to see you again," Emily lied. Matt said nothing.

Beth was one of the worst people that they'd ever had the displeasure of meeting, and Toby wasn't much better. They'd met her at Emily's thirtieth birthday party, when Jen had taken it upon herself to extend an invitation to several friends who turned up empty-handed, drank Emily's house dry, and left in the early hours after keeping the neighbours awake and throwing up in various spots around the house.

Beth had spent half the evening lamenting to Emily and Matt the injustices of the court system because she had just lost full custody of her four-year-old son to her ex, who she described as a piece of shit. She complained emphatically about how the guy no longer had to pay child support, and that she could only afford to feed her kid toast on the weekends she had to 'babysit' him. Then, in the next breath, she bragged about the bag of cocaine she had saved up to buy for herself, produced it from her back pocket, and then Matt had spent the rest of the night panicking about the wellbeing of their much-beloved cat after he'd seen her brandishing her cocaine-encrusted fingers under its nose.

He was also sure she was the one who'd raided Emily's jewellery box.

Toby, who wasn't in a relationship with Beth at the time, had got blind drunk within two hours and then gone on a homophobic rant, and followed it up with some good, old-fashioned racism, just in case anyone was in any doubt about his character. To top it off, he'd made some remark about their house smelling rotten before he left, which had made no sense until a week later when their house did indeed start to stink. They'd found oranges and bananas – presumably stolen from their own kitchen – stuffed down behind several of their radiators.

"I don't think we've met?" Toby said, eyeing Matt.

"I'm the guy who threw you out of his house for being a dickhead," Matt shot back, without missing a beat. "So, Jen. We waiting for anyone else? Any other nasty surprises lined up?" His tone was outright hostile, but Jen feigned ignorance and poured herself more wine. There were empty glasses in front of Emily and Matt, but Jen didn't extend the bottle to them.

"There's no need to be so rude."

"Isn't there?" Matt, who had so often insisted that Emily shouldn't let Jen get a rise out of her, was taking the bait all too easily.

"Interesting tattoo," Emily cut in, addressing Beth. Her desire to dispel the tension before it escalated further was – she had discovered in therapy – a co-dependent compulsion that she tried to reign in, but couldn't. Not when she was with Jen. Beth smiled and turned her arm so the back of it was flat on the table, fully displaying the symbol she wore on her wrist.

"It's a brand," Beth corrected her, tracing her perfectly manicured fingers over the scarring. Emily didn't know what to reply to that – she wasn't up to date on the most recent alternative trends. Jen said she'd gone 'mainstream', whatever that meant. She leaned forward and smiled with what she hoped looked like sincere interest. The brand looked familiar, but she didn't place it until Matt tapped her knee under the table and nodded at the weird markings painted on Jen's wall. Sure enough, Beth's brand matched the one at the centre. Emily stared at the wall, realising that the symbols weren't painted on, but etched in.

"I've got one too!" Jen piped up, twisting in her chair and lifting her hair off the back of her neck. It was the same symbol, only Jen's was still healing. It was red, mildly blistered, and looked sore. Emily was commenting in her mind about the fact that of course, when someone else was paid a compliment, her sister felt the need to divert the attention onto herself. While she was passing that judgment, Matt was tapping her knee again. She looked at him, finally seeing that he was not only tense, but worried.

"I think we should go," he told her in a whisper. But Joe heard him.

"You're leaving already?" He was sincerely disappointed.

"Our wires must have got crossed somewhere," Emily rushed to explain. "We thought this was a dinner and we haven't eaten all day."

"It's not crossed wires, Em. She specifically invited us for dinner and now we're sat here with a stranger, a thief, and a racist. It's like the set up to a bad joke." Matt was pushing his chair back while Emily quietly fumed that he'd felt the need to expose her attempt to just get out of there without a fuss. Joe hurried to stand before Matt made it to his feet.

"No worries, man. I'll whip up a snack!" He sauntered off towards the kitchen, patting Matt's shoulder so hard on the way past that it forced Matt back into his seat.

The kitchen was behind them, so neither Matt nor Emily noticed that Joe passed right through it and out of the room.

"I said it was a gathering," Jen lied. "You probably just assumed dinner because you're always hungry." She flashed an open-mouthed smile and a giggle at her other guests. "Carb Queen. That's what I call her!"

"Babe..." Matt took a deep breath in, swallowed, closed his eyes. "I'm not feeling good, can we please just go?"

"Such a drama queen," Jen declared. "You've been hanging out with her too long. You're just hangry!"

Joe returned and took his seat, smiling as he laced his fingers together. He and Toby exchanged a look, and then Toby stood to pour everyone a glass of wine. As he did so, his shirt sleeve pulled back a little, and Emily noticed the edge of the branding on his arm. She looked at Matt, who was now glaring at Jen, glad he hadn't seen it. She was beginning to feel deeply unsettled, and not in the usual way that Jen tended to elicit. She dared not voice it for fear of sounding paranoid, but the instinct that something was not only amiss, but somehow dangerous, was screaming at her.

"I'm popping to the bathroom," she declared, rising from her seat. *And then we're leaving,* she thought, but didn't say. Something was telling her that voicing the intent to leave would somehow make actually leaving more difficult. Her stomach rolled over, rumbling with both hunger and anxiety as she ventured through the only other door, into the downstairs bathroom.

She pressed a hand to her mouth as she shut the door behind her, wondering if she might actually throw up. It was pitch black in there with the door shut, and she fumbled for the light switch. Once illuminated, she realised why the small, pristine room was so dark. The large window was boarded up.

She approached it, reached out and touched the wood, almost expecting her fingers to graze air, so strange was the sight. The window hadn't just been boarded over – it had been done so with a kind of effort that didn't fit the possibility that it was just a temporary measure, in the case of, say, the window being smashed somehow. Three long, thick panels of wood, placed one on top of the other without even an inch of space between them, were nailed into the wall, ruining the paintwork on either side. Emily ran her fingers over the nails, wondering what else looked wrong here, and then realised. They weren't nails, they were screws. Jen – or more likely Joe – had not merely nailed some boards across the window, they'd drilled into the wall and screwed them in.

Jen could be weird, but Emily couldn't fathom what would possess her to wreck a wall in her precious house to do this. An answer surfaced, whispering insidiously in her ear, but she pushed it away. There was no reason to get paranoid. Only, that wasn't true, was it? Because it never turned out to be paranoia with Jen, it turned out to be reasonable cause for concern one hundred percent of the time.

Back at the table, Emily tapped Matt's shoulder. "Let's go."

"Thank God," Matt mumbled, getting up. For some reason, that elicited a chuckle from Joe.

"Emmy?" Jen looked hurt. Emily looked at her once, decided not to bother justifying their exit, and turned with Matt towards the exit. "Em!" But whatever spell Jen had cast over Emily their entire lives was suddenly broken. Emily had no idea what the hell kind of stressful weirdness was coming up, but what she could always bank on with her sister was that there *was* stressful weirdness on the way. Matt had been right, he always was, and she not only recognised that but finally felt ready to accept it.

No one went after them and they reached the foyer peacefully, the mere sight of the door enough to start relaxing Emily, because she was now sure that this was the last time she would ever leave Jen's house.

"You were right. Sorry for dragging us here," she said to Matt, who was holding her hand and one step ahead of her.

"It's fine, babe. Let's just get out of here." But when he tried the door, it wouldn't open. It was locked, and the key had been removed. They both turned, inspecting the key hook on the wall next to the door, and then the several small decorative tables around the room, but there was no sign of the keys.

"Oh, for fuck's sake," Matt muttered, turning back towards the kitchen. "Jen!" As if in a trance, Emily trailed behind him. That feeling that bowing once again to her sister, being lured back into her chaos, was somehow dangerous this time was rising up out of the pit of her stomach. Her eyes swept the foyer as she left it, this time not just noticing but questioning why all of the other doors were shut. She glanced up to the bedrooms on the landing, which were also all standing closed.

Matt was only seconds ahead of her but by the time she caught up with him, he was already heated well past what she thought his boiling point was.

Jen, Toby, and Beth were standing in a line against the back wall, the creepy painted symbols hovering above them like sigils. They were muttering in unison, though Jen couldn't make out the words. Joe was leaning against the kitchen counter, his thumbs hooked into the belt loops of his trousers, smiling at them.

"Let us out!" Matt roared.

"Just relax, have some wine," Joe chuckled.

"Fuck off!" Matt shot back. "I'll relax when someone opens the door."

"Don't be scared," Jen said to Emily, and she really did sound like she was sincerely trying to soothe her. "This is a scary step but things will be better after."

"After what?" But Emily knew what.

"After. We just go to sleep and when we wake up reborn, we'll have the power to change the world." It was the sincerest that Jen had ever sounded, and that worried Emily more than anything else her narcissistic, self-serving sister had ever said. Emily's eyes went to Joe, to the oven next to him with no flame inside, though the interior light said there should be. She noted the oven door sitting slightly ajar. She looked at the gas burners, unlit, though all four of the knobs were turned to their highest settings. Back to Joe, who was smiling at her now. He shoved his hands into his pockets, winked.

"What are you on about?" Matt demanded. Colour climbed into his pale cheeks but drained away as quickly as it appeared. He looked ghastly. Emily grabbed his wrist and took him with her to the sliding patio doors, moving quickly enough to alarm him.

She threw the heavy black curtain back in a hurry to get to the doors. If they were locked, she'd smash them open with one of the dining chairs. A sound escaped her, even though her lips were pressed so tightly together they had turned white.

These doors weren't locked. They were no longer there. In their place was a freshly plastered wall so newly built that it was the only part of the room unpainted.

"What the hell?" Matt pressed his hands against it in disbelief, unable to comprehend what he was seeing or why.

"We can have everything we want," Toby breathed. "We'll be given the power in exchange for our sacrifice."

"Jen, this is nuts," Emily turned to her sister, her expression imploring her to see sense. "Whatever he's roped you into," she gestured to Joe, whose eyes were still on her, "it's a lie."

"Let me do this for you," Jen breathed, an almost identical mimicry of the way Toby had just spoken. "We've had a rough ride, Emmy. But we don't have to be powerless, we can have everything we want."

"Remember the time you joined that Evangelical church?" Emily reminded her, desperate to evoke the right perspective to snap Jen out of Joe's bullshit. "That turned out to be an actual cult?"

"That was different," Jen argued, the placid yet somehow smug expression disappearing from her face. "I was indoctrinated. You can't hold that against me."

"I'm not holding it against you," Emily assured her, having to slip into an act of her own now. A performance that implied the complete opposite of what she was actually feeling – that she wanted to slap and shake her sister into sense, flee her dark tomb of a house, and then punch her lights out afterwards. "I'm just saying..."

"Joe has shown me the way."

"Us," Beth corrected her. "It's true, you guys. He's shown us his own power. He's already made the sacrifice."

"Em, what the fuck is happening?" Matt whispered. His face was blanching now.

"They're poisoning us," she replied, gesturing to the cooker. It took Matt a second to realise what she meant, but when he did, he charged forward towards Joe.

"Uh-uh-uh!" Joe shook his head, pulling a lighter from his pocket. Matt stopped in his tracks and Emily flinched back against the new wall. "I could just use the ignition on the cooker, but it'll look so much cooler setting fire to the air with the flick of a lighter instead, don't you think?"

"Joe!" Beth giggled, looking from Jen to Toby. When she saw that they weren't laughing, she stopped. "That's not what we're doing."

"I think it i-is!" Joe said with a sing-song rhythm.

"I don't want to do that," Toby said. "You said it would be painless."

"You said we'd just go to sleep and then ascend," Jen added. The worry in her voice made Emily feel sick.

"Ascend." There was a second, and then Joe actually threw his head back and laughed. The branded trio looked at each other, their faces dropping into masks of impending terror.

"You're not really going to set us on fire?" Jen's voice was trembling.

"I think I will."

"Why?"

"Because it's hilarious. Look at your faces!"

"Will we still be reborn?" Toby asked. Joe replied with more hearty laughter.

"I will. You? Not so much. You're my gifts to them."

"I trusted you," Jen said, betrayal engraving itself into her face, possibly for the first time. Emily would have laughed at the irony of Jen having the audacity to be hurt by a lie, all things considered, if it weren't for the severity of the situation.

"That's on you," Joe chuckled. When he next spoke, he addressed each of them in turn. "Well, this has been fun, and I'm sorry to cut it short." He looked at Matt and Emily. "I was hoping to mess with you two – the branding ceremony is always hilarious to me – but I knew as soon as you walked in that I couldn't get you on board. Well..." he looked at Emily, "maybe you. But definitely not you," he finished on Matt. "Bombs away!"

"N—" Emily didn't even get the whole syllable out before Matt flicked the lighter open. The very last thought she had was that this was Strike Three.

They all burned.

THE END

Dead

Grace knew that she was dead the moment she sat up, on account of the fact that her body did not rise with her. It just lay there on the laminate flooring. She allowed herself a moment to register that her top half was upright, and her bottom half was still just sitting there inside her hips and legs, and managed to draw herself back from the edge of panic. *Worry about what you can control* – that's what her boyfriend, Eric, always said when she was spiralling into anxiety. Though, to be fair, anxiety usually struck because of an unusually high bill, or that weird sound her car randomly made. She had never woken up dead before, and that seemed like a more severe problem.

She breathed deeply – or rather, went through the motions of it. Quite proud of her composure, despite having to climb out of the rapidly cooling meat of her former self, she got to her feet and tried to recall her last moments.

She'd been bleeding out, she remembered, although it didn't take Sherlock-level skills to work that one out. There was a rather enormous and unsightly pool of her blood, the last drops of which were trickling from a dirty wound on her neck, and it was still spreading. So, quite recently dead then, she deduced. But what happened before that?

Her body was flat on its back, feet pointing towards the closed cellar door. Ah yes, that's right. She had been running up the cellar stairs for some reason, hurled herself in a full circle so she could slam the door behind her, and then she had just collapsed backwards. She didn't remember hitting the ground, so she'd either fainted from blood loss or just died on her feet. At the tender age of thirty-five, dying from a gushing neck wound wasn't how she thought she would go. Ideally, she'd hoped to go out on a mega acid trip, at the ripe age of ninety or so, after consuming copious amounts of all the drugs she was too afraid to try. Whilst skydiving into a pit of snakes. Something like that, something cool. This was just a mess. But why? She stared at the cellar door, straining to decipher the weird noise that was floating up from the cellar. Shuffling?

"Oh my God." It was all flooding back to her now.

She'd been renovating the cellar.

It was a small, dank room with bare, plastered walls, and the ugliest floor tiles to ever curse the planet. They were orange and brown, and placed in no particular pattern, so there were clumps of brown with an orange thrown in and rows of orange with one or two brown tiles shoved in at the ends. It was the most disorganised floor pattern she'd ever seen, and a blight on the rest of her new home, which was old but otherwise modernised and decorated in that pristine 'showroom' type of way. She'd thought the cellar a jarring oddity in comparison with everything else when she'd viewed the property, but it was the only thing she hadn't liked, so she figured it could be fixed.

And there she had been, fixing it. Eric had suggested just leaving it alone – they didn't need the space for anything and in his opinion, it just wasn't worth the time, money or effort. Plus, he'd added, Grace had never renovated anything before. She'd only just learned, after replacing a broken one, that there was more than one type of tin opener, and she'd had to go online to figure out how to use it. She had scoffed at the insinuation that just because she was inexperienced, she couldn't figure out how to lift and replace some goddamn tiles by herself. If it were not for the perceived slight, she probably would have hired someone, but the implication that she couldn't do basic household improvements seemed like a challenge, and she had never been one to turn down a challenge. That's why, only a week before, she'd eaten that worm. Admittedly, it wasn't her most clever trait.

She'd managed to get about half the tiles up, but *that* had been much harder than YouTube had had her believe, and she'd mangled the job. There were halves and bits of tiles still firmly attached to the ground all over the place. What they'd been fastened with, she wasn't sure, because she was a secondary school English teacher with no building expertise. She had found a layer of what seemed to be old, unlevel concrete underneath what she'd managed to remove, and it was coming up in bedraggled clumps and bringing loose dirt with it every time she yanked up a tile. It also had to go. The whole floor had to be redone. Why had she even started this? Oh yeah, because the rest of her house was perfect, and knowing the cellar wasn't bugged her. She was a completionist, that way. She'd once spent four and a half hours trying to steal a flute from an ogre on a video game, just because she'd successfully robbed every other boss of their treasures and she couldn't accept the failure of one annoying blip on an otherwise flawless thieving spree.

Beneath said concrete layer was packed dirt. When she'd hit that, she'd looked at the badly-built wooden staircase that led up to the ground floor and wondered if this cellar was even part of the original build, or if one of the previous owners had just picked a spot and dug down to create it. It certainly appeared that way. Why anyone would "decorate" the floor – if that's what you could call the attempt – and do nothing to the walls was a mystery she didn't have time to ponder on. She was just grateful because, judging by the horrid job they'd made of the ground, they probably would have insulted the walls with some hideous wallpaper had they bothered to finish.

She'd gone too far to admit to Eric that this job wasn't in the same league as repressurising the boiler, and she'd sat on the bottom step drinking her thousandth cup of tea that day, observing the mess she'd made, wondering what the next logical step was. And then the dirt had moved.

It had risen like something shifting just beneath the surface. She might have dismissed the movement as bad lighting playing tricks on her eyes had it not so vividly reminded her of the film *Tremors*. She'd stood up, ready to bolt upstairs, thinking that perhaps a burrowing rat was about to appear, and then the earth rose into a point and crumbled, revealing an elbow as it broke through the surface, and then a forearm, and a desperate, clawing human hand.

"Jesus Christ," Grace muttered, rising to her feet, dropping her mug. It smashed to pieces on a surviving tile, but she barely heard it shatter as she was already halfway to the person who was desperately trying to dig their way out of her cellar floor.

Had she been watching a film, she would likely have been yelling at the protagonist to get the hell out of the cellar, for whoever was buried there must have been there a long time. Something was amiss. But, as she threw herself to the ground in a bid to help, she wasn't really thinking anything. That was the thing about a high emotional state – it shoved logic right out of the top-floor window. All she knew was that someone was in dire need of assistance, and time was of the essence lest they suffocate. Of course, if her brain had been engaged, she would have realised how far away that ship had already sailed. It was likely on the Australian coast by now.

"I've got you!" she cried, pulling the stray arm with one hand and trying to dig around it with her other one. A second hand broke though, and she abandoned the digging and grabbed it, standing up and pulling with all her might. A head emerged, the eyes, nose and mouth all clogged with dirt, its hair so clumped with mud that it barely looked like a human at all.

Afraid of pulling the poor soul's arms from their sockets, Grace let go and dropped down to a crouch, slid her arms around the person's torso beneath the armpits and yanked backwards. Surprised by her own strength (maybe she could fix the floor down here by herself, after all!), she freed the panicked burial victim and they fell backwards, Grace on the bottom and her new friend on top.

Grace breathed heavily with relief as the said friend scrambled to get up, only that's not really what they were doing. Instead, eyes still glued shut with dirt, it lunged right into Grace's face. She turned her head, a squeak of surprise escaping her, as its mouth bore down on her cheek. She closed her eyes against it and pushed back.

"I have a boyfriend!" Grace yelped, trying to angle her knee into her admirer's crotch, where she hoped to find balls. A swift blow there would stop them, but if it was a vagina situation, she had no idea. She'd never kneed anyone in the vagina before and didn't know if it had the same effect. Her knee connected with something, but it made no difference.

Dirt cascaded from its open mouth into Grace's eyes and pattered across her face. It went in for a second attempt, this time its mouth freed of most of what had been packed in there, and clamped its teeth on her neck.

Grace screamed and bucked her body as violently as she could, rolling to the left and, for just a moment, even further *into* the bite, but she succeeded in toppling the thing off her. It grabbed at her as she clambered over it, but its fingers barely grazed her, and she threw herself towards the staircase, pressing a hand to her neck.

She swayed halfway up to the ground floor, her blood pulsing out of the wound against her palm, spurting through her fingers as she desperately tried to stem the flow. The fact that her heart was hammering in her ribcage like the enthusiastic subject of a pinball machine didn't help. She tried to calm herself down, hoping to slow the blood escape rate, but it was impossible while sprinting to safety. She was seeing dark spots as she reached the top of the stairs, and the colour green was seeping in from the corners of her vision. And then, finally reaching the ground floor, she'd spun and slammed the cellar door, and the sound of it slamming was the last thing she heard.

Staring down at her body now, Grace felt a little fed up. How unfair that she would be essentially chomped to death when in the act of trying to do a good deed. Also, she realised as she gazed down, she had wet herself at some point during the ordeal too. As if bleeding out all over her new laminate flooring wasn't bad enough.

It was stupid that she flinched back when she heard someone coming in through the front door a moment later, on account of being dead and all. How much worse did she really expect this to get? Besides, it wasn't some random house burglar entering the small foyer that she stood all ghostly in, it was just Eric getting home on his lunch break.

"Babe!" he yelled into the ether, "chuck the kettle on!" He stopped, his eyes dropping to her body on the floor, to the blood. The colour drained from his face like someone had pulled a stopper out of his neck. "Grace?"

"I'm dead," she explained, but he didn't acknowledge her. He took a tentative step forward, looking down at her, his eyes as wide as saucers.

"Grace?" he repeated, and then much to her disbelief, he asked, "Are you alright?" Oh Eric. He never had been the sharpest tool in the shed, though she supposed she was quite the hypocrite thinking him stupid, considering she had enabled her killer to kill her.

"Eric, hello?" she approached him, waving both arms. "Can you see me?" But of course he couldn't, because she was a ghost. Must be. How else would you explain waking up in your own dead body? "Oh, great. That's just great," she sighed. She thought about every ghost film she'd ever seen, how the common rule was that ghosts couldn't interact with the living or move objects unless some shouty dickhead on a train taught you how. This was going to be shit.

Trembling, Eric took one last long look at her still corpse, her wide-open eyes that stared at the ceiling, and then side-stepped her and went into the living room, taking care not to step in the blood. She heard him unzip his jacket pocket and then he started speaking to what she guessed was an emergency operator on the phone. He sounded so sad, and now so was she. There was quite a lot she hadn't done in life. She'd never done a skydive, never had a child. She'd never learned how to make decent fried rice, and that one really irked her. She could never get it to the right consistency before frying it. *Oh God!* And she hadn't returned that library book.

Forlorn, she looked back down at her body, hating it for so quickly pumping all of her blood out onto her new flooring, and then a glimmer of hope shot through her when the fingers of her left hand twitched. The hope rose like a phoenix ascending from ash as her eyes moved across the ceiling, and she sat up.

"Oh, thank God!" she gasped, smiling. But as quickly as the smile arrived at the prospect that she wasn't dead after all, it slid from her face at the realisation that if that were the case, then she would not be standing here, a literal ghost of her former self. "Oh," she muttered, as her body clambered to its feet. "Oh no." Her body turned towards the sound of Eric's voice and started shambling towards the living room. "Oh no!" she screamed, as her body set its once brown eyes, which were already turning a bit milky, on to her beloved boyfriend. Her body lunged into the lounge.

"Grace, I thought you were..." Eric's relief trailed off and he started screaming. Grace raced in behind herself, trying to slap at her back, but to no avail. While her transparent hands didn't pass right through, they made no impact whatsoever. Her animated corpse couldn't feel the attack any more than she could feel her ghost hands attacking – there was no sensation whatsoever for either of her.

"Get off him!" she screamed, still trying in vain to help Eric, whose right cheek was already detached and being chewed inside Dead Grace's mouth. Though already sitting on the couch, Eric somehow managed to collapse off it onto the floor in a pool of his own blood – there was now, frankly, a ridiculous amount of blood all over their pristine house. His eyes rolled back as he landed face down on the carpet, and then they closed. He was still breathing when Dead Grace settled on her knees over him and started to eat his shoulder.

"Ah. Ugh." Grace was sure that were she still alive, the sight of her feasting on Eric's flesh like that would have made her sick.

The eating went on for quite a bit, and Grace couldn't believe that every now and then, Eric emitted a groan that indicated he was still alive. Once again, the unfairness of it all struck her – she was bitten properly only once, and that had done her in, but Eric had been getting chewed on for ages and there he was, still amongst the living.

A car horn outside eventually broke Dead Grace out of her snacking frenzy. The sound of it alerted her to the outside world, distracting her from the apparently tasty morsel that was Eric. She rose and turned, plodded back into the foyer, past Ghost Grace, and made towards the open front door. Eric, in his shock, had never closed it.

"Oh shit!" Ghost Grace exclaimed, following Dead Grace. The car that had summoned her to the great suburban outdoors was long gone, but the nice old lady crossing the road with the aid of a walking stick wasn't. Wait, scrap that – it wasn't a *nice* old lady, it was Marge, the next-door neighbour. Ghost Grace and Dead Grace saw her at exactly the same time. "Oh God. Oh no..." Ghost Grace, despite knowing she couldn't physically stop herself, tried anyway. She followed behind as her dead self approached the unsuspecting old battle axe, whose thin, narrow back was to them. Her sense of anticipatory dread deepened when she realised, ten feet away, that it was fairly quiet out on the streets, and Marge was helpless.

"Marge, look out!" Grace screeched at the top of her voice. Marge, as usual, didn't acknowledge her presence. She was a little deaf. Also quite ignorant, and not a fan of what she referred to as 'the youth', which was anyone under the age of fifty. Ghost Grace passed her shambling corpse and stepped in front of Marge, frantically waving her arms and pointing at the bad guy behind her. "It's behind you!"

Oh no, it isn't! her mind – littered with childhood memories of pantos – shot back. She giggled a little, composed herself, remembered that Marge was in mortal danger.

Eight feet and closing, and Marge was still crossing the road. She was only five feet from death when another car came, stopped, and honked. Despite the greater issue, Grace had to wonder what kind of asshole beeped at a little old lady who struggled to walk with a stick.

Marge turned towards the car, actually shaking her fist – God, Grace loved that generation for things like that – and then in her peripheral, saw Dead Grace. She turned to face her.

"You look like hell," Marge said. "And *that* is unlady-like." She pointed. Ghost Grace flushed as she followed Marge's pointing, shaking finger to the wet patch at the crotch of her jeans. That was somehow more embarrassing than her gore-splattered face and torso. "Grace, what are you doing?"

Dead Grace kept approaching, her arms now outstretched, her fingers bent into claws. Marge reacted by clutching her handbag ever tighter. Ghost Grace was pretty insulted by that.

"I knew it! You young people are all the same – no respect!" Marge concluded, and swiped at Dead Grace's ankles with her stick, tripping her. Dead Grace landed in a heap in front of the stopped car, and instantly jolted forward, teeth-first, onto Marge's open-top loafered foot. This was becoming a nightmare.

Grace wondered if ghosts could get headaches, because she could swear one was setting in.

"Ah!" Marge screamed, and brought the stick down sideways, knocking Dead Grace's head away. She stumbled back, almost lost her balance, regained it, and then as quickly as she could, made for the pavement, where their other neighbour, Rashid, was exiting the corner shop, newspaper in hand. The front-page headline read '*Blood Rain – Global Warming or Hoax?*' Grace, who usually ignored the news, was actually interested for once, but there was no time for reading right now.

"Will you get off the goddamn road?" The asshole honker was out of his car and approaching the Graces. What was presumably his wife watched from the passenger seat. Two kids peered around her head from the backseat.

"Get back in your car!" Ghost Grace yelled, but it would have been too late even if she were audible. Dead Grace clamped onto his shin, allowed easy access to his leg on account of the shorts he was wearing. Ridiculous choice of outfit – it was January, for crying out loud. She tore a chunk out of his calf. He screamed, stumbled back, hit the ground. Dead Grace was on him, at his throat. Ghost Grace flung her arms in the air in annoyed defeat, rolling her eyes to the sky.

"Larry?" The wife, also now out of the car despite seeing the danger.

"Oh, for God's sake!" Grace complained, stepping in front of the woman, who passed right through her on her way around the car to her flailing husband. It was an eerie feeling for both of them, apparently, as the wife shivered. She reached her husband and then just stood there screaming, not helping. Not running, just screaming. Practically offering herself up as fodder. Grace had to wonder why she'd bothered to get out of the car if she was just going to screech.

"Get back in the car!" Larry yelled, echoing Ghost Grace's thoughts. He was fighting Dead Grace off and pretty successfully despite the gash in his throat.

The scream of children from behind them.

"Oh, now what?" Grace sighed, turning in the direction of the commotion. Several children were gathered and screaming near her house, from which Eric was emerging with that disgusting milky look in his eyes. "Just run away!" she exclaimed. Several of the kids did run. Two just stood there clutching each other and screaming. She wondered if she was seeing the principle of survival of the fittest in action, then wondered why she was having such callous thoughts, then wondered if this is what happens when one becomes a ghost. Either that, or literally everyone in the vicinity were idiots – screaming idiots that just stood there when the better option was clearly to just run away.

The car door slammed and she'd barely time to turn around before the asshole and his wife drove right through her and down the street. Dead Grace was unperturbed by the escape of her second course – she was already ambling up the road towards a delivery man carrying a parcel.

"Mrs. Ellis, what are you doing?" It was Rashid. Ghost Grace turned in time to see Marge drop her cane and reach for him. Even from her view of the back of Marge's head, she could tell the old woman's mouth was wide open. Rashid was gently pushing her back by her shoulders. "I'm very flattered, but you're old enough to be my...argh!" Marge had lunged, apparently unencumbered by her former frailness now that she couldn't feel her arthritis.

The kids' screaming turned to gurgles behind her. Ghost Grace couldn't look. Then the screech of tyres, the enormous sound of metal smashing into brick, and she whirled back around to see the asshole and his wife had crashed through someone's front garden and right into the external wall of their house. Through the car's rear window, she could see that the asshole was attacking his wife, teeth first.

The owner of the home that was now adorned with a crumpled car – a woman in her sixties who was affectionately known by everyone on the street as 'Nannie' because she liked to bake for everyone – shot out of the front door. Ghost Grace didn't bother shouting this time as Nannie yanked open the driver's side door. The asshole turned his attentions on her, and she ran screaming – bitten on the wrist – back into her house, without closing the fucking door behind her. The asshole, his corpse of a wife, *and* the reanimated kids clambered out and followed her, and then there were screams. Ah, of course, it was Wednesday – Nannie's book club.

Rashid shuffled across the road in front of her. He had an arm off. Ghost Grace turned, looking for Marge, wondering how in the hell she'd managed to pull that one off. The back of Marge's fluffy, permed head disappeared into the corner shop. Of course, her arrival brought a beat of silence, and then more screams.

Ghost Grace raised her arms in defeat for a second time, helpless to stop the chaos that she herself had unleashed. Was everyone that her corpse, and subsequent victims, encountered not only doomed, but contagious? And why was she the only ghost? Maybe it took a while to... materialise? She really had no idea how long it had been between her death and her reappearance.

She looked up the road to her shambling self, watched as Dead Grace tripped over the parcel the delivery man had abandoned. He was already a mile away, sprinting in the opposite direction. Perhaps he'd learned to bolt from years of having to deliver goods to people who kept big dogs out front. She decided not to bother following herself anymore; it was depressing and embarrassing. As well as having the munchies that only human flesh could satisfy, she was splattered with blood, had wet her pants, and now her top was ripped and one of her nipples was poking out.

Resigned to the reality that there was really nothing she could do about any of this, Grace turned back towards her house, wondering if she might find Ghost Eric in there. She half-hoped she wouldn't – he was insufferable when he was right and she wasn't in the mood to explain that she should, as he'd insisted, have just left the cellar alone.

THE END

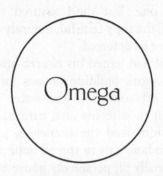

Omega

"*They will be punished with everlasting destruction and shut out from the presence of the Lord and from the majesty of his power...*"

Thessalonians 1:7-9

Pastor Bob looked out at his flock, then beyond them to the curious people that had started to slow and stop, in anticipation of some sort of performance or display. Maddie watched his thin lips curl into the same smile she'd seen a thousand times by now, but instead of comfort, for the first time ever, it struck her as off. *It's just nerves*, she told herself. This was a big day – a special day. The most special day she would ever have.

She glanced around at the rest of the congregation, a small but enthusiastic group. There used to be more of them, but over the years, members had fallen away, either from the church or their faith entirely. Pastor Bob blamed social media; said it was one of the Devil's tools to spread lies and doubt, possibly his most powerful one. But (he'd assured those who remained) the truly faithful, the truly dedicated, could never be deterred.

Maddie had joined his church after hearing of all his work building houses for the poor in worse-off countries, the water wells he'd helped put in with his own bare hands. She'd watched him feed the homeless, joined him on trips to hospitals to spread hope and love to the terminally ill, personally house and help to rehome several spouses and children of abuse. But, as noble and wonderful as he had proven to be time and time again, that wasn't why Maddie had stayed so loyal. It was the other things.

Firstly, there was the healing. There were many naysayers who'd written the most awful things about Pastor Bob: they said he was a greedy crook that took advantage of the most desperate, perpetuating the ridiculous lie that he could heal their ailments. The thing was, Pastor Bob had never taken money from anyone. He was the only church leader amongst the many that Maddie had known over the years that wouldn't accept payment for his services, or even donations for his church. *What does God need money for?* he'd reply when asked about it. *What do I need money for?* And yet, he healed them.

So many times, outsiders assumed and accused him of planting people in his audience, people on the inside, in on the hoax, to be "healed". And the thing about *that* was, Maddie knew that wasn't true either. She'd taken her great aunt with her to church once, a woman who had been paralysed from the waist down since a decade before Maddie was born. Pastor Bob put his hands on her, and within thirty seconds, the woman was walking.

He'd cured a church regular of a speech impediment, extracted another's terminal cancer, eradicated blindness, and removed the affliction of Alzheimer's Disease. And Maddie had seen it all – known each and every one of those healed before and after. He was no fraud.

Secondly, and more importantly, Pastor Bob had a direct line to God. The Almighty warned him of things, and he in turn warned those in the church. He had foreseen so much that had then come to pass: a huge earthquake spanning several Welsh valley towns that had never before suffered an earthquake, their homes and businesses crumbling to dust and crushing those poor, unsuspecting souls as they came down; a tsunami – the scale of which was hitherto deemed impossible – that wiped out the population along one entire Australian coast; inexplicable fires that raged across Germany – origins unknown – taking half the population. And so many more.

Maddie had listened from the same pew each time as he recounted, in minute detail, what he'd been shown, and then within a week, the horrendous incident would come to pass. The world as they knew it, Pastor Bob told them gravely, was in its last days. God's wrath was upon them: free will combined with the inherent evil of man had risen so despicably that God could no longer abide it. Hell was coming for most, and those who fell into the good and gracious minority would be reaped.

Only when she had boarded the hired minibus with the rest of the congregation was she informed that The Reaping was today. So much sooner than any of them expected, despite the horrific natural events and the man-made atrocities rising and worsening all around the globe. It was today.

She'd begged to turn back so that she might bring her family and fiancé with them, and she wasn't the only one. It was too late, they had to go now, their beloved leader had insisted. But there was nothing to fear because those who were true of heart would be saved, wherever they were, and they'd all soon be reunited. A clear half of what was left of the church got off the bus then. If they were to be saved regardless of location, they'd argued, then they'd be with their loved ones when it happened.

Maddie caught Pastor Bob's eye as he scanned the crowd, her mind conjuring a silent plea for him to notice and eradicate her nerves, which had struck her suddenly and inexplicably. She had followed the man from childhood to – literally – the end of the world. Words once spoken by her fiancé – *ex*-fiancé – slipped into her mind.

There's something off about that guy. It had irritated her beyond belief that the first and only time Billy had deigned to show up for one of the hundreds of church events she'd asked him to attend, he'd felt the need to speak ill of Pastor Bob, a man who'd been the closest thing she'd ever had to a father figure. It irritated her even more now that his paranoid opinion was wriggling around like an earworm inside her head. She shoved her discomfort aside, deciding that it wasn't about Pastor Bob at all – it was about the fact that she'd reluctantly ended her relationship with the love of her life five days ago, and the bastard didn't give a damn. He hadn't called, hadn't sent a half-hearted text. Hadn't even replied to any of hers – hell, he hadn't even opened them.

Of course things felt off right now. Her heart was broken. But if Pastor Bob was right, she'd only have to endure the pain of that for a few more minutes, and then everything would be awash in His glory.

"My brothers and sisters!" Pastor Bob raised his arms until his hands were level with his head, palms facing outward. "It's time." The congregation ceased all talk immediately, and the muttering between the outside observers quietened some. Pastor Bob's smile became a wide smirk, just for a second, before it smoothed out into a more natural and friendly expression. Once again Maddie heard Billy's words in her head, and the already-present knot in her stomach twisted.

"Those of us who have lived good lives according to His word are about to rise into the Heavens and be saved. Those that used their free will to spend their days indulging and spitting in His face will be left here on Earth..." he brought a closed fist to his mouth and coughed into it, but Maddie saw the corners of his mouth and would have sworn on the Bible that he only did so to cover a chuckle "...to burn."

Maddie turned her head to look at Rose beside her. Rose was already staring at her, her knitted eyebrows matching Maddie's.

"Is he laughing?" Rose whispered, facing forward again as if to check what she'd seen with her own eyes.

"Of course not," Maddie lied, more to herself.

"Yes he bloody well is."

Maddie faced forward, determined to disbelieve her instinct that something was very very wrong here all of a sudden. She was a woman of intense faith and to let that go – even only a thread – would be her unravelling. Pastor Bob continued his rambling diatribe about the souls that would be saved in the reaping, and appeared to take a lot of pleasure in elaborating on the fire and brimstone that would rain down on everyone else. She had never seen the side of him that was emerging, but it was probably just the excitement of what was to come that was amping him up so much.

"He's never steered us wrong, Rose. Never." It was true.

"He's acting weird," Rose replied. That was also true. *Don't say it*, Maddie thought, but Rose did. "Off."

There's something off about that guy.

"I'm starting to wonder if Billy didn't..."

"Don't, Rose."

"...didn't have a point, after all," Rose continued, talking over the interruption.

"He's got us this far," Maddie insisted, unable to take her eyes off the man who had practically raised her, who gesticulated wildly in his continuation of his speech about all those evil folk who would die screaming in flames.

"I don't like this," Rose said. She'd stopped whispering and was looking around to see if anyone else was listening, and moreover, agreeing with her. "I'm leaving. I don't like this."

"Please don't go," Maddie said, tearing her eyes away and back to Rose again. She reached out and clamped her hand on Rose's wrist, an action that was met with an initial look of surprise, and then annoyance, as Rose twisted out of her grip.

"Look, I've never had as much faith in him as the rest of you have, especially you."

"But don't you believe?"

"In God, yes," Rose replied. "But about being reaped? All this fire and brimstone stuff? I don't know. And the things he's saying now..." she pointed at Pastor Bob without looking at him. "I don't want to be associated with this."

"Rose, please. I'm scared." And it was true, she was. Her best friend stared at her for several seconds and then heaved out a sigh.

"Fine." She took Maddie's hand and held it tight.

"It's time!" Pastor Bob bellowed, and now he was grinning from ear to ear. His hands were pointing down at the floor, and he lifted them slowly to the sky. Before Maddie had time to question what was happening any further, she was being lifted. They all were.

There were gasps and excited mutters, some joyful sobs, from those in her clan. There were gasps and screams from the spectators, some of whom were also rising. Those who remained firmly on the ground were backing away, getting their phones out to record the spectacle. A few of them started running.

Maddie looked down at her feet, at her dangling toes that now pointed downward with nothing but air directly beneath them. She squeezed Rose's hand, held it for dear life. It was ice cold, just like hers.

They were rising slowly, but at four feet above the ground, the icy fingers of fear stroked at the bare skin on the back of her neck. Though the destination would be worth it – it *was* Paradise, after all – being drawn up so excruciatingly slowly like this was already accelerating her heartrate. It was like that theme park ride where they take you up up up and then dangle you over a deep, dark abyss for what feels like forever before dropping you into it. Only this was worse, because she could see the ground, could see how high up she was going. She'd always been afraid of heights.

She tried to swallow the lump that was rising in her throat, her eyes brimming with tears, mad at herself for having any fear at all during what was actually a wonderful moment – the most beautiful she could experience in life. She looked down at those watching from the street, at all those who would suffer and perish instead of receiving the gift of salvation. There were so many of them. Surely, they couldn't all deserve such a fate? *That* fate. Did anyone, really?

She raised her eyes to Pastor Bob, who was of course rising with them, his arms reaching out to the sides. *Like Jesus on the cross*, she realised, not without concern. It was, at best, in bad taste to mimic the Messiah like that and, at worst, some sort of insult. Blasphemous, even.

"Don't fear! Soon, you will be in his warm embrace!" Pastor Bob declared, his eyes sweeping his faithful sheep. They landed on her, locked eyes with her, and then he did something he had never done before: he winked. Even in mid-air, now twenty feet above the ground, Maddie flinched at the gesture.

"Behold His power! His glory!" Pastor Bob bellowed, and then he erupted into laughter. The whole congregation was staring at him. Not at their dangling feet, not at the ground as it inched away from them. The way he was laughing was somehow stranger than the rest of it. Several seconds later, a couple of them started to laugh with him. It was part discomfort, part amusement, part curiosity – but all of them were desperate for it to end.

Pastor Bob laughed and laughed, his head thrown back and dangling, and then eventually as he composed himself, he faced them again.

"Pastor Bob?" one of the elderly congregants directly before him asked.

"You stupid fucks," he replied, and then started laughing again. Murmurs, whispers, concern. Fear. Maddie looked down at the ground, at least fifty feet away now. Her stomach flipped at the realisation. The air was growing colder. She looked back up to her apparent saviour again. Her mouth had dried up. She swallowed and licked her lips, instantly feeling the sting of the cold threaten to chap them.

"I can't believe the shit you people will swallow just because it comes from a guy in a white collar!" Pastor Bob was gloating, mocking them. He pulled off his collar and dropped it. Several of them watched it flutter down to the ground where they had not long ago stood. It would take a short while to get there. "Are you guys nuts?"

"But... we're being reaped!" someone squeaked from behind Maddie. She thought it might have been Ethel, the oldest and by far the sweetest member of the church. The poor woman had outlived not only her husband, but both her children. Her daughter had been ill, and her son had been involved in a traffic accident.

"Reaped!" More laughter from good old Pastor Bob. Maddie's eyes were saucers as she stared through her fellow church members at him, at this man whom she had followed, eating up every word, for so much of her life. He had either undergone some sort of personality transplant in the last five minutes, or he was the most duplicitous snake on the planet.

"We're ascending!" That was Adam Perry, a man whose voice was ordinarily as commanding as his presence, but now it was little more than Ethel's frightened, insistent squeak.

"We're *ascending*," Pastor Bob formed air quotes as he said it, "because I thought it would be fun. Honestly, the look on your faces!"

"No." Ethel again. "This is just a test of our faith. We're being tested." There were several murmurs of desperate agreement, despite Ethel's complete lack of conviction in what she was saying.

"You think so?" Pastor Bob smiled at her, and dear old Ethel dropped. Maddie turned at the woman's scream, the sound of absolute terror – the first time she'd ever truly heard that sound in real life – and watched her flail as she plummeted mercilessly. She stared up at Pastor Bob with enormous pleading eyes, both hands reaching out to him for a lifeline, for any mercy, but he gave none.

She landed on both feet, obliterating them. Both ankles sprayed out blood and bone in several directions. Her left leg snapped sideways at the knee, the rest of her exploding like a water balloon as it made contact with the concrete.

The entire congregation screamed and wailed. Several of them were sick, their vomit raining down on the bystanders who were also reacting with shock and horror below. Maddie, her mind rapidly emptying of any coherent thought, noticed several of them were still filming. Their phones were in their hands but they weren't calling emergency services. They were livestreaming the death of a wonderful, ninety-something year-old woman, whose last moments had been terrible and the complete opposite of what she deserved.

They were over one hundred feet in the air now. Several of them were hugging themselves, shivering.

"Devil!" someone far braver than Maddie shouted. Pastor Bob shrugged and smiled, as though he had been caught doing no more than cheating a hand of poker. "God will save us!" The righteous man plummeted to his death. This time, only half the congregation watched his descent. The rest either couldn't bear to see it or were too afraid to take their eyes off their tormentor, lest they be next.

"Pray tell, faithful sheep: what the *hell* makes you think that there even *is* a God?"

"Isn't there?" Adam, his voice smaller and meeker than ever. Pastor Bob shook his head, laughing. *No.*

"There's only us," he told them, and he was so pleased to do it. Several of them burst into tears – most of them trying to hold back the sound and failing.

"But if there's evil, there has to be good. If there's you, there has to be angels." Adam flinched with every word he spoke, as if trying to will them back into his mouth, to unspeak them.

"Devils. Angels." Pastor Bob grinned wider. "Same thing." He stared at Adam, who squeezed his eyes shut in response, expecting to fall. He didn't.

"There is no Heaven, only Hell. There is no God, only us. And – and this is the best part..." he paused for dramatic effect "...there is no eternal rest. Only suffering."

Maddie turned her head to the ground, rendered mute and unable to think past the grief that was crushing her. It was all a lie, and she'd lived according to it. She'd sacrificed her time, her prospects, and the love of her life, to live by this. So high was she that those beneath her were ants, but she had never felt lower.

Adam fell, his scream piercing Maddie's thoughts. Rose's hand trembled in hers.

"Look," she whispered, and Maddie turned her head to follow her friend's gaze. There was another group off to the east, hovering in mid-air, almost as high up as they were. Too far away to make out their features, but close enough so that Maddie could see that they were all facing their own robed, emphatic leader, eating up his every word. His every lie.

"Maybe this really is just a test," Rose pleaded with herself. But Maddie, for all her years of devotion and faith, could not believe that, not when the evidence so strongly suggested otherwise. She averted her gaze, unable or unwilling to watch the first of the other group fall... or maybe their Judas would dispense with the theatricals and just drop them all at once?

She faced the west instead. And there they were, another group midway through their own ascent. No one noticed the sob that burst out of her, the pouring tears that she'd managed to hold back until now. They were all too focussed on Pastor Bob, on begging for their lives. She scanned her own small crowd, her chosen, extended family, her heart breaking a thousand times over as those who were close enough clutched each other, and those who weren't wrapped their arms around themselves.

"There are so many," Rose mumbled, her head twisting in all directions. Maddie responded by grasping her hand with both of hers, vowing that no matter what, she would never let go. If this was to be their end, she would not allow him to separate them, to force them into their last moments alone. Rose was shaking violently.

Several more of their flock fell screaming. Every time one of them went, both Maddie and Rose flinched. There were only four of them left.

Their leader held the last of them suspended for so long. He was enjoying it. He held them for so long that by the time he grew bored, there were dozens of congregations in the air. He held them for so long that they had to watch at least half of those groups plummet to their deaths.

Despite the altitude, the air grew warm, and then hot. Maddie and Rose felt it in their chests first, as they gasped in small breaths of air. It was uncomfortable, and then only seconds later, painful.

"What's happening?" a small voice from somewhere behind them.

"It's okay, honey," her dad lied. And then they too, were gone. Maddie and Rose looked at each other, both of them struggling between the need to breathe and their reluctance to scorch their lungs. It was as if the oxygen itself had ignited.

Sirens below. An explosion somewhere off to the south, a plume of thick, black smoke rising from the north. And the screams of those on the streets – a rising cacophony of bewildered panic, and then all-out terror. The wind carried the sound up to them, as if they even needed the reminder that the ground was no better than where they were.

They looked at each other, grasping each other's hands.

A plane sailed by overhead on its merry way, and then a few miles on, inexplicably plunged from the sky. Maddie watched it go. Rose didn't; her eyes had been squeezed shut for a while now.

She couldn't bear to see the Pastor's eyes on her, though she could still feel them.

And then, Rose was dropped.

"Please!" Maddie screeched, feeling the sudden weight of Rose's body in her own two, small hands. She clamped tighter, crushing her fingers against Rose's hand, desperate to save her. Rose's eyes sprung open impossibly wide, her pupils enormous. She swung her free hand up, unable to reach Maddie's arms and settling on her thigh.

"Don't drop me!" Rose cried, her voice so shrill the words were almost impossible to understand. Maddie sobbed as Rose slipped out of her grasp. "Don't drop me!" she repeated, over and over again. She was out of Maddie's hands and falling. The arm she'd manage to encircle Maddie's thigh with slipped down past her friend's knee, and she clawed at her foot in a last-ditch attempt to save herself. But she couldn't. All in less than a single second.

Maddie's body racked with silent sobs, her chest tightening painfully as she watched her friend plunge to her death. The guilt of failing her and letting her die, *killing* her, was too much. Too much. But she wouldn't feel it for long.

"See you on the other side," the Pastor said. "Forever."

And then, Maddie fell.

THE END

The End

What comes after death is a question that's been on the lips of mankind since you slithered out of the ooze of creation. Even before you evolved language, you stared up at the stars and wondered what was out there. Before the age of communication, when you were all scattered in your tribes and towns, with no idea that so many of you even existed, you had that in common. The curiosity of what comes next, the difficulty accepting that perhaps there's nothing at all, the denial. The arrogance in your disbelief that you – yes you – in the grand scheme are but a grain of sand that will be swept away with the tide, like all the others. Forgotten. Insignificant.

Half of you think death is the end. And of that half, most of you are fine with that prospect – at peace with it. Live a great life, dream and accomplish, help people, gather wealth, be selfish, be unselfish, leave the world with those who knew you weeping, or pretending to. A comparatively small number of you, those that don't believe in an afterlife, struggle with it. It hinders the little you have: you see the days rushing by, your birthdays swinging around too fast, the sum of your contributions ultimately worthless. Most people are not born great, even fewer forge themselves into greatness, so what you give will, in the end, be meaningless. You will have no impact. You wonder, what is the point?

The other half of you dream that death is just a gateway to something bigger and grander and more wonderful than anything you could imagine on Earth. You picture fluffy clouds with fat cherubs, harps, and wings. You think you're destined for an eternity of whatever you want, all that you never gained in your mortal life. You dream of being reunited with all you loved; you dream of luxury – the kind of luxury the vast majority of you could never afford before. That's all most of you really want and desire – to *have*.

Do you have any idea how few of you think of Heaven as a place to give, to help, or spare a thought that perhaps it's a place for those who actually need it? The idea of Heaven, as you envision it, has always been so amusing to us. It used to be a place of peace, but you've turned it into a place of things. You, as a species, became impossible to satisfy as soon as the word *more* entered your language.

The greed.

How many of you ever really considered Hell? You joke about it, work it into your fiction as a place that can be escaped or avoided. You re-interpret the texts you claim to follow to fit your agenda – to end up in the light, fluffy place, and not the other one. *As long as you believe, God will accept you,* you assure yourselves. And we laugh when you do that, because instead of following the perceived rules, you break them but still demand access to an eternity of pleasure.

Most of you don't deserve Heaven. A lot more of you should have been more concerned with Hell.

So, now that your mortal life is at an end, what happens? Because with all your ideas and hopes, none of you ever really know until you get there. And there is a *there*. A *here*. You're here now, with us. Now, you finally know that there isn't just nothing.

But you'll wish there was. You'll wish to be insignificant. You'll wish you were just allowed to be forgotten.

There is something, there is an eternity, and you have reached it. Here's the big secret – life was the reprieve. You think you suffered? You don't know suffering. But you will.

You see, there are no scales. There's no cosmic balance, no yin and yang, no karma, no imaginary sorting system that divides you into the worthy and the irredeemable, no spiritual system that sends you to one place or the other. Because – and this is the best part – there is only one place, and it's where you will be from now, forever.

The truth about the end is that there is no end.

Salvation and damnation? One and the same.

God and the Devil? One and the same.

You all end up with us. What you "deserve" doesn't factor in.

Perhaps the nihilistic sceptics of you are right, perhaps there really is no point to anything you do. May as well be greedy and live to serve only yourself. Or perhaps the reality of what comes after makes your lives more meaningful than anything else – maybe it's all that matters, because it's your only shot to do good, be good, help those who need it, and sleep well at night.

You won't be sleeping anymore, not ever again.

Where are you now? With us. And what is this? Hell.

Your concepts of Hell have also amused us, more than your concepts of Heaven. We've watched your iterations, laughed at your depictions. Some of you imagine fire and brimstone, eternal torment and suffering. Some of you imagine being forced to relive your worst day over and over again forever. Some of you imagine that it's just eternal boredom, perhaps standing in a queue that never moves, for the rest of existence. That one gives us a kick. Only the most privileged of you could conceive of Hell as mere banality – you've no concept of suffering. We'll change that.

What happens to you now?

We'll bind you and burn you with fire and
acid, flay you and stretch you and break
you.

> We'll sever your limbs, slew the flesh from
> your bones, and chew on your nerves as
> they come through.

We'll cut you and bleed you and gouge at
your eyes,

> yank your nails from their beds as we
> whisper our lies.

We'll promise to stop, to offer reprieve,

> Then we'll use our bare hands to deglove
> and desleeve.

You'll beg and you'll scream and you'll wish
it to end,

> but it won't. You will never transcend.

When we've torn you to pieces and you
think we're done

> you'll become new again to continue our
> fun.

You will have no rest, no sleep, no break,
no time to think or dream,

all you'll know is pain forever, you won't
even scream.

You can't get used to torture, you can't
hide inside your mind,

and if you try, we'll just burrow and follow
you inside.

We don't get bored and we never tire,

we're not like you, we drink of fire.

We show no mercy.

We *have* no mercy.

This is forever.

This
Is
The End.

Also by Kayleigh Dobbs:

Collections
Corpsing (Sinister Horror Company, 2017)

Visit Kayleigh Dobbs at her website:
www.happygoathorror.com

*Now available and forthcoming from
Black Shuck Shadows:*

Now available and forthcoming from Black Shuck Shadows:

Now available and forthcoming from Black Shuck Shadows:

blackshuckbooks.co.uk/shadows

Milton Keynes UK
Ingram Content Group UK Ltd.
UKHW041025271123
433339UK00004B/49